Dancing Under the Same Moon

☯

Debraha Watson

This book is a work of fiction; names, characters, and incidents are products of the author's imagination. Any resemblance to actual events or persons, living or dead, is entirely coincidental.

Published by My Vision Works, Farmington Hills, MI 48334

Copyright © 2010 My Vision Works Publishing

All rights reserved. No part of this book may be used or reproduced in any manner whatsoever without the written person of the author.

Printed in the United States of America

Library of Congress Cataloging-in-Publication Data

Watson, Debraha
Dancing Under the Same Moon written by Debraha Watson

1. Fiction
2. Women's Studies
3. African American

ISBN: 1453766456

Dedication

Acknowledging the Creator through which all things are possible and to those who continue to walk with me on this tedious journey called life ... Yohanis, Jamila and Kay, much love!

Acknowledgement

I am blessed to have so many positive, creative and loving people in my life. Thank you, Ronnie Jones Boggess, for your guidance, patience and belief in my work. I am grateful to all of my sister friends ... you know who you are. I am blessed to have the friendship, listening ear and editorial expertise of Dr. Harriet Slocum and Marie Bell. To all of my fellow scribes out there toiling to have their work published: Keep writing ... keep believing.

Author's Note

This book, while a work of fiction, came alive through the voices and characters that presented themselves to me while I slumbered and slept, daydreamed through meetings, or stared out at the moon on a sleepless night. They came talking, crying, laughing and singing. They came demanding that I tell their stories. Twilight came first, ten years ago to be exact.

She formed as I was researching my past in preparation for writing my yet unpublished memoir. She is a composite of the stories I heard about my mother and grandmother, who were called "root working" women by people in the small town of Cinderella, West Virginia. She manifested herself physically one day as I was walking down Fenkell Avenue, in Detroit, Michigan.

In the distance, I saw a woman walking towards me ridiculously dressed in a red chiffon dress from the 1960s. She had a worn, vintage mink stole, the kind with the whole animal attached, draped around her shoulders. It was ninety degrees that day. She smiled and nodded as she walked past me. I thought to myself, "poor chile." After I entered the hair salon, Ms. Mary stood staring with her mouth open holding hot curlers in mid air. I felt a presence behind me. Turning I stared into her penetrating eyes. She said God had given her a message for me. She delivered it, waved goodbye and disappeared as quickly as she had come. We laughed and talked about her for hours. Her presence and message stayed with me for years.

Whenever I publicly read Twilight's story, the audience would ask what happened to her baby. A year or two after writing Twilight, I wrote the original story of Legacy. The writing was forced and I didn't "feel" her as I usually do with my characters. I packed away the story in my junk drawer, promising to get back to it. Another year passed and a friend who had asked me over breakfast inquired if I had finished the story about Twilight's baby. No, I said, I can't get into it. Unable to sleep that night, I sat listening to the hum of the refrigerator and other night sounds, and she came to me. I wrote the first draft of her story nonstop. I was surprised when she described herself and even more surprised when she introduced Pearlie. I finished both pieces as the characters competed and negotiated for my time.

Tuck came next. He walked in while I was vacationing in Northern Michigan. It was another early morning and I sat drinking bitter tea watching the sunrise. My mind drifted back to my childhood as I thought of the junkman, fish man and repentant wino who were part of the tapestry of my eastside Detroit neighborhood. They became Tuck, or he channeled them.

By now I was asking myself a question: Who was this other person that I felt had not come forth? She remained hidden for several more months. One Sunday while sitting in the movies, Mattie Mae Lemons finally showed up. I wrote on a crumpled up napkin her first words: "*I found a body hanging from the rafters* ...." She shared her story and went back into the lives of the others, filling in the blanks.

When I shared the completed work, some tried to categorize it and put it in a box. My intent is that it gives a universal message of love, loss, pain and redemption. Hopefully, it will stir us to reflect on and change our own biases. As we all know, writing is an art. I chose to preserve the vernacular way of speaking, the use of dialect, and to take us back to a time when we were just plain folk who had a good old time with storytelling. I believe in celebrating the power of language, and I am glad to be able to capture my work in print. I look forward to hearing from you and so do Mattie, Pearlie, Twilight, Legacy and Tuck. They are watching us. Laughing and dancing under the same moon.

Mattie Mae

Chapter 1

I found a body hanging from the rafters of Momma Appie's barn when I was seven years old. I stood staring at the figure, its head slumped to the side, face all twisted up, eyes bulging from the sockets. I was frozen there, caught in that space and time. I heard Momma Appie calling me to supper. I moved my mouth, and at first nothing came out but air. Then the fog lifted from my head, and I saw her face put back in place. Her eyes dancing just like the last time I saw her. My soul escaped from my mouth as I screamed *Momma!*

Aunt Talla heard my screams and, grabbing a hoe, came running, thinking that I had been cornered by that ole rattler that had been seen around 'bout the house earlier. She snatched open the door of the barn and a stream of light beamed down on Momma. Aunt Talla hollered like a wounded animal and fell to her knees, pulling me down with her. She buried my face in her bosom and called on Jesus. Others came running; a crowd formed with rumblings and prayers falling from their mouths. Uncle Brother broke through the crowd and without ceremony cut the clothesline from around Momma's neck. Her body fell to the hard ground like a crumbling mountain. There was deafening quiet except for Momma Appie's humming.

Before that afternoon in the barn, I had not seen Momma in more than two years. She had run off with Mr. Turner, a traveling musician. I heard Aunt Talla cussing after Momma left, saying Mr. Turner had already left behind an infirmed wife and six hungry children. She said he would leave Momma too after he used her up.

I remember the evening she snuck off. It was after my grandmother, who we all called Momma Appie, went to sleep in her favorite rocking chair sitting by the fire. I always rubbed her tired, knotted-up feet as she hummed and mended clothes or read her Bible. She always fell off to sleep in that old chair after humming and talking to no one in particular about the day's events. Momma tiptoed into the house, making sure Momma Appie was asleep. She was all dressed up in a powder-blue suit that hugged her shapely body. Her hair was freshly pressed and pinned up, with large waves framing her face. I grabbed and held on tight to her long, delicate fingers as she handed me two peppermint sticks. She pulled away and patted me on my head.

She said, "Now, Mattie, I'm going to be going away for a while ... make us a better life. I'll come back soon with a trunk full of pretty dresses and ribbons."

I told her I didn't like dresses and ribbons, but she said, "Hush chile, all little girls like pretty things like dresses and ribbons." At that she opened the door and slipped away into the darkness of night.

When the sun rose the next morning, I told Momma Appie what my Momma had said. She looked away, staring into nothingness and started humming. Then she said, "I reckon you be with us awhile."

Momma Appie's house was often full of people. Her baby sister, Aunt Talla, who she had raised like her daughter, had three children. They all lived with us off and on. Momma Appie had six men-children, as she called them, and my Momma. She said my Momma was her only girl and only heartache. I often spent time at Momma Appie's when my Momma went off chasing her dreams, and I loved playing with my uncles and cousins. Most often I bunked with my Uncle Herman, who was the same age as me. My other uncles were much older, with Uncle Brother being the eldest and the "man of the house."

He didn't like me being there. In fact, he hated it and told me so every chance he got. He was the one who told me that I came feet-first into the world. Ass-backwards he called it. Said I was made and born up at Mt. Vernon Hospital for the Negro Insane over in Mobile County. He said my Momma was found clawing in the dirt after she went limped brain and attacked a white woman she worked for with an iron skillet. She told them she did it 'cause the woman called her a lazy, ignorant nigger.

Truth was she never landed a blow. The woman's husband wrestled the skillet from out of Momma's hands and beat her with it, breaking her arm and nose. She somehow got away, dazed, and they found her late in the night talking crazy with her eyes glazed over. They hauled her off to jail, but not before beating her some more. From there they herded her off to Mt. Vernon.

Momma made the local newspaper, and Momma Appie saved the yellowed clipping in a faded, white beaded bag that she so loved. She had Aunt Talla read it to us from time to time like a bedtime story.

"A negro woman employed by Mr. Franklin Walsh on his plantation about four miles outside of town created considerable excitement and alarmed the surrounding community with her ranting about seeing 'haints' and the Holy Ghost. For her own safety and the safety of others, she was taken to Mt. Vernon Hospital for the Negro Insane."

Chapter 2

The newspaper story and Uncle Brother's version of what happened varied considerably, but every Negro in town knew the truth—they beat her brains out. My Momma was locked up in Mt. Vernon for four years. She had been in and out of my life all my life. I guess that's why I couldn't cry at the funeral. She was buried with just the family present, real quick. Momma Appie said she was where she always wanted to be, floating among the clouds and dancing around the moon. She looked real serious when she said the book of Momma's life was now closed, but mine was open to do good things. I had to keep on going.

So it was. I was raised by my grandmother Appoline Lemons in a household of six of her men-children until I was fourteen years old. Momma Appie was kind but stern. She provided as best she could, and she made all of us do some kind of work. I'd rather work than go to school, so after a while she got tired and gave up on me and what she called book learning. She said, "You'll learn all you need to know if you keep on livin'."

So I tagged around with my uncles, learning how to build and fix things. Of course, some of Momma Appie's church folk took exception to this and started whispering about her mannish granddaughter.

"Look at her, always running around wild, wearing men's clothes, cut off all that long, pretty hair, her best asset ... walk like a cow in a muddy field with them men's boots on ...."

I heard them talking but they made me no never mind and I kept about my business.

Then, the summer I turned fourteen, Momma Appie slept away from here. For the first time in my life, I cried like a baby. Uncle Brother, who had been gone for years up North in Chicago, came riding back to town in his fancy car, chest all poked out, saying he come to settle things.

After the funeral he found me at my favorite spot—sitting beside the creek that ran along back of the house. He stood over me like a grizzly bear chewing on a tree twig.

"I reckon you know I ain't taking care of you. In fact, Momma Appie let you set in this nest too long. You best figure out what you goin' do, quick. I be leaving in a few days." With that he walked on down the hill looking for pleasure and bringing trouble.

I had never seriously thought about life until then. When Momma Appie was alive, my life was continuous, safe. But right before she died, she told me out of the blue, "Mattie, life is hard on us women folk—you best get use to it."

I pondered my next steps. Uncle Brother, true to his word, sold the house right from under us. My other uncles moved on and into the lives and houses of lonely women. As for me, my choices were limited. I spent that summer doing odd jobs here and there, making enough for a decent meal once a day. I lived under the moon and stars. If the weather turned bad, I'd steal away in a barn or deserted shack.

I did this for months, growing tired in mind, body and spirit. One night as I was sleeping under the stars, Momma Appie came to me, warning, *"You best watch sleeping on that cold, hard ground. You catch consumption, snakes get you, ain't safe out there exposed to the world. You need to find you a safe place—come out of this here wilderness. Get up and get down on your knees and let Jesus whisper in your ear."* She faded into the sky, smiling.

Fully awake the next morning, I knelt down and listened. There was nothing but the sounds of nature: critters scurrying under the leaves, birds in flight, greeting the world a good morning. In the distance I heard that ole mean, one-eyed rooster crow on the Coleman farm. I got up, dusted the dirt and dry leaves off my pants legs and felt hunger kick me in the stomach. Gathering up my knapsack, I swallowed my last handful of goobers and drank water from the creek as I washed my face. I looked out into the world, trying to figure out my next steps.

It was such a beautiful morning that I found myself walking aimlessly into the woods. I came out on the other side, drawn to soft, sweet organ music. Before I knew it, I was walking into the doors of a little white country Methodist church. Heads turned as I walked in. My eyes were glued to the preacher, a thin, carefully dressed colored man in a black suit and spit-polished shoes. He smiled and nodded a sign for me to take a seat. I sat down, crammed between two big women wrapped in heavy green-and-blue shawls despite the warmth of the early morning heat. I suddenly became aware of the smell of my unwashed body, raggedy overalls and muddy boots.

I looked out over the seated multitude. My eyes ran up and down the pews, taking in the congregation. There were stiff-collared men who looked like someone dug them up from the cemetery. There were young devils who I had seen on Saturday nights keeping up an ungodly rumpus at Miz Delia's. Then there were the mothers of the church who, let them tell it, already had their place picked out in heaven; and, of course, the younger sisters who looked at the young devils as potential husbands.

I was so busy people-watching and daydreaming that I paid little attention to the sermon. I do remember that the preacher said, "Though times might be hard right now, we have to pray and hold on. A new day was coming and we best be ready."

At the closing of his sermon, the music drifted through the church and I followed the notes, which seemed to dance in the air, to the woman playing the organ. Our eyes met and she smiled. My heart jumped around in my chest so hard I thought it would work its way up and out of my mouth.

Chapter 3

After services, I hung back away from the crowd, watching her graceful movements. She had a lovely face, with a pointed chin and bright, dancing eyes. I watched her pretty, thin lips as she worked her way through the crowd, talking and smiling. Her hair was slightly frizzy from the heat and worn high on her head like a crown. It highlighted her exquisite face. She wore a blue dress with a lacy bodice that framed her narrow waist and long, swanlike neck.

As I was staring, trying to memorize every inch of her, the two sisters in the shawls grabbed me by my arms and hauled me off to the back of the church where food was being served. They plopped me down between them and handed me a plate piled high with country ham, potato salad, fried chicken, pickled okra and cornbread. I buried my head in the plate, coming up for air only long enough to swallow a cup of sweet tea and belch.

"Oh my," said the sister with the green shawl to the

other, "this chile is starved. Son, when was the last time you ate?"

I had often been mistaken for a boy; and I noticed that the older I got, people was more hostile about it when they found out I was really a girl. So I just smiled and mumbled, "thank you, gotta go," as I worked my way out of their grip and ran back into the woods.

That night I dreamed of a queen in a blue dress. I saw her every time I closed my eyes that week, which led me to do something I had never done before and something I have regretted ever since. I stole. I watched ole man Coleman load his truck and drive off down the road while his wife and children headed to the fields before I snuck onto his property. I took a clean shirt and pair of overalls off the clothesline. Then I went into the house and stole a box of soda, a washrag and a piece of cold corn bread.

I ran off into the woods and prayed that Momma Appie would forgive me. She once told me she despised a thief. It was the worse thing you could do was to take something that somebody else had worked hard for. I pushed her words out of my head as I bathed in the creek, using the soda to clean my body and teeth. Afterwards, I rubbed mint leaves and lilacs all over my damp body, and I slicked my naturally curly hair in place with my own spit.

Walking gingerly, I found myself back at the church. This time I arrived early, so early that besides the preacher I was the only one there.

"Glad you came back. Come here, son, set up front," he beckoned. I was nervous and ready to run, when he said, "I got to put some finishing touches on this sermon, do a few things round back. You alright to sit here and we'll talk after service. You got away from me last week."

"Yes, sir," I said weakly. I sat there staring at the cross over the pulpit and imagining my love sitting at the organ. Just as I thought it, there she was—standing so close I could smell her vanilla scent and peppermint breath. That day, she wore yellow and looked like Momma Appie's freshly baked lemon pound cake.

"Well, looka here, you came back. Glad to have you. Hope you enjoyed the services last Sunday. I didn't catch your name the last time."

My tongue had swelled, but I managed to gurgle, "My name is Mattie Mae Lemons."

"Well," she said all drawn out, "Miss Mattie, my name is Mary Elizabeth Jackson. Reverend Little is my daddy." At that I looked puzzled, wondering why they had different names. She read my mind.

"I'm a widow, lost my husband last year in a mining accident in West Virginia. That's where he was from; we lived there for five years. I never set roots there though. Alabama was always my home; so when he died, I come back here. I figured since Momma died, Daddy needed my help. I also teach piano and organ to the local children. You got nice, long fingers—you ever think about learning to play?"

"No ma'am," I said. "I like to do manual work."

"I don't remember seeing you around the schoolyard," she said. "Where you been hiding?"

"I quit after the fourth grade, never took to it. My Aunt Talla taught me to read a little bit and do my figures at home. The rest I learned from my grandmother. Momma Appie never went to school a day in her life, and she was probably smarter than you."

No sooner had the words fell out of my mouth did I want to take them back. Mary Elizabeth smiled at me like I hadn't said nothing and asked me, "Where is your Momma?"

"She in glory with Momma Appie, I reckon. It's just me," I told her.

"Just you—you rather young to be out here on your own. How you making it?"

Before I could answer, Reverend Little called, "Ma'y Elizabeth, come here and help me set up for communion." At that she disappeared, like the sun going down.

Like the Sunday before, I didn't pay much attention to the sermon. Instead, my eyes were glued on Mary Elizabeth. I watched her long fingers dance over the organ keys, and this time she sang. I never heard such a voice, seen such a beauty.

After the service she grabbed my hand, and we went out back. This time, she fixed our plates of food and told me to follow her. We moved away from the crowd and found us a private place along the dusty road where the trucks and cars were lined up. Mary Elizabeth grabbed a blanket from the back of one of the trucks and spread it out on the ground under the old oak tree. She patted a spot for me to sit down.

"Whew, this Alabama heat—born and raised here but sometimes I still can't take it." She squinted at the sun and started talking. She told me about her family. The hurt she felt like none other when her mother died. Her brothers and sisters, who had married off, and her arranged, peaceful, loveless marriage to a man twelve years her senior. He was also a preacher, a friend of her daddy's.

She talked about "crosses to bear," family secrets, stuff that I didn't understand at the time; but I sat smiling, just wanting to be in her presence. Watching her chew her food brought me such delight. Then she turned and looked me in the eye and asked, "How old are you, Mattie?"

"I'm fifteen," I said.

She thought for a minute. Then she said, "I was a year older than you when I married—still a baby—I'm almost twenty-five." At that I raised my brow and she smiled.

"Well, truth be told, I'm twenty-one, be twenty-two in a couple of months, but I feel like I've lived a lifetime already."

I didn't like the fact that she saw me as a baby. "Well, pardon me, ma'am, but I ain't no baby," I said defensively.

"I been taking care of myself for more years than I can count. Even when Momma Appie was alive, I fended for myself. She had her hands full with my no 'count uncles."

At that she contemplated for a minute and then said, "I guess inexperienced would be a better description. It can be trouble out in the world for women like us."

I creased my brow, not sure of what she meant. Before I could ask, her daddy was calling for her again. She got up, straightened out her dress, looked down at me and said, "Meet me back here at nightfall."

She then marched across the road, heading back to the center of the church activities. I sat watching her until she disappeared over the hill. I picked up the chicken bone that she had left on her plate and gently sucked the marrow out of it.

Chapter 4

I sat there for a while trying to sort out my feelings as I watched people leave the church picnic. The sun was beaming down full force. The ants and flies were feasting on the dried-up food that was left behind. I shooed them away from our plates as I cleaned up and walked off to the edge of the woods to escape the burning heat of the sun. I scraped the food from our plates for my invisible friends and kept walking down to the creek where I had left my meager belongings. I washed the plates, shoving them inside my knapsack.

I then stripped off my clothes and bathed once again in the cool water. Allowing the sun to dry my body, I sat naked on a boulder staring at my reflection in the stream, trying to sort out what life held in store for me. Later, unable to find an answer, I slipped into my clothes and wandered back to our spot at the foot of the tree. I lay down on the soft blanket that Mary Elizabeth had left and waited, chewing my nails and trying to quiet the butterflies fluttering in my stomach. Finally, the heat of the sun and sheer exhaustion settled in, and I dozed off into a deep sleep.

I was awakened by the chilled air and the faint scent of bread pudding. It was dusk and standing above me was the silhouette of an angel. I rubbed the sleep out of my eyes to make sure I was fully awake.

Mary Elizabeth stood in the spotlight of the moon smiling. She extended her hand towards me, delicate gossamer wings beckoning me to rise up and be enfolded into the comfort of her arms. Finding a familiar place, I looked down into her face as her lips rose to mine. Lost in soft feathery kisses, I found home and followed my instincts as I slowly unbuttoned the bodice of her white-laced blouse, revealing her plump breasts. In a blanket of flames we moaned in delight and expectation, unwrapping our gifts to each other. Magically, we found the cover beneath us as my mouth followed my fingers over the landscape of her body, tasting raw brown sugar.

As the night unfolded, I learned things about myself that were always on the surface, just never exposed. When the sun rose the next morning, I was completely in love. I followed Mary Elizabeth around like I was a hound dog and she was soaked in chicken grease.

It took some convincing, but after about a month her daddy let me stay in the back room of the church in exchange for cleaning and minor repairs. I heard him more than once talking to Mary Elizabeth about his concerns that I had "mannish ways," as he called it. She assured him that she was working on teaching me to be a lady as well as preparing me to accept Christ as my personal savior, which was why we were spending so much time together.

"After all, Daddy, she was raised in a house full of men without much of a woman's presence," she explained.

On another occasion I heard him remind her about her past sins, as he called them, and cautioned her that I might be the Devil's temptation.

"That was a long time ago. A mistake ... I am sorry that I hurt you and Momma and brought shame on the family. That's all behind us now," she told him.

That seemed to pacify him for a while. But I always tell people, you live a lie and sooner or later it will catch up with you, and it did.

Chapter 5

Two years passed easily—I noticed that Mary Elizabeth wasn't as enthusiastic about me as she first was. In fact, she was acting towards a new widower in the church like she used to act towards me: smiling, attentive, fixing his plate and such. She took to caring for his two little girls, making them dresses and giving them piano lessons. I felt her easing away and I fought back by making myself more visible when he came around.

Mary Elizabeth said that my presence annoyed her, and this caused more distance between us. Finally one evening, unable to take it anymore, I exploded, telling her I felt her drifting away. I would never let her go.

She calmly stared and then said, "Surely, Mattie, you didn't think this could go on forever. I'm a mature woman; I must secure my future. Mr. Foster has asked me to marry him. He needs a momma for his girls. He's not that bad. In fact, Daddy says he's got a good savings set up.

Another thing, I think Daddy suspects the nature of our relationship. I can't hurt him again, Mattie. Don't you see, this will be good for us both. Nothing has to change. We can still be together; we just have to be careful."

I felt a stab in my heart with each of her words. Tears welled up in my eyes, but I refused to let them fall. I couldn't control my voice, which was weak and trembling, as I said, "Well, I guess it's settled. You goin' marry Mr. Foster—I guess I'll be on my way."

With those words, it was her turn to scratch and claw. She dropped to her knees, begging and crying, "Mattie, don't do this!" She grabbed at my pants leg, whimpering like a scared dog, "Mattie don't leave me … we can do this together … nothing changes."

I kept walking 'til she shook loose. I left her there under that same tree, an altar of our love, scooping up the dirt from my footprints as I walked broken into the night.

Mary Elizabeth married her Mr. Foster. After that, I wandered around for seven years, living and learning. Looking back now, I can thank her for helping me to know myself and giving me a place to live. I continued to open myself up and take lessons from life and the people I met along the way. I been hurt, and I have left some broken hearts in my wake. I fancied myself a free woman, come and go, play as I pleased.

That is until the day I walked upon that field of golden flowers. That was the day that I met Pearlie. It was like I knew her before in some other time, like she was a part of me that I couldn't be without, like a heart or liver. Just one glimpse of her and I knew it. I know some folks don't believe in love at first sight, but I'm here to tell you that's what happened. And it was different than with Mary Elizabeth—she was in my life for a season, helping me to find myself.

With Pearlie, I knew she was my lifetime love—there was never any doubt—though she was scared for a while that ole Cleon would come out after her. I told her he wouldn't, and in time we settled into life together. They say true love comes around only once. You have to be open to see it when it shows up. I was a woman walking around without much purpose; that is until Pearlie came along. Thankfully, we had a lifetime to dance together under one moon.

Pearlie

Chapter 6

I was brought up to be a good colored girl. My Poppa was the grandson of Mr. Warren Barber, whose daddy owned up most of Attala County, including my ancestors. Poppa was the spittin' image of ole man Barber, and his one ounce of Negro blood was well hid save for his voice. There wasn't a white man on Earth that had a voice as rich and full as Poppa's. His deep baritone voice gave him away.

I never knew any of Poppa's people. They had all disappeared into the fabric of life by the time I came along. His Momma and Poppa worked themselves into an early grave—the war took his two brothers away. Only one came back from across the sea, and I heard stories that he wasted away in the fast life of New York City. His only sister, Corine, beautiful, pampered creature that she was, gave all her love away. She was ate up by what my Momma called the "nasty" woman's disease; so that left

Poppa alone as a young man, trying to fit into a world where no one wanted him.

White folks hated him because he reminded them of the sin of the South, and many colored folks scorned him because of his natural brilliance, which they called his uppity ways. To add insult to injury, Poppa was packaged in white skin with grey eyes and silken blond hair. Poppa was a fine specimen of a man. He stood nearly six feet tall, had a strong muscular neck and broad shoulders, and a perfect set of pretty white teeth. Momma always said it was his smile and those teeth that stole her heart.

Momma's people were the Woodsons, a wild, rowdy bunch. She came from a family of thirteen children—she landed smack in the middle, which is how she came to raise her last six brothers and sisters after her mother died and her father stole away to start another family. Momma was all of five feet two, nutmeg brown with long, jet-black hair that she kept hard pressed. She had a nervous habit of biting her nails and twisting her thick locks of hair around her finger. The strain of caring for her family had drained her spirit and zest for life. Poppa said Momma radiated unease.

Her only solace was the church, where she went three days out of the week. This is where Poppa first saw her the evening he preached his trial sermon at Christ Temple Apostolic Church. He said while all the other sisters danced and threw themselves in his arms, lost in the spirit of the Holy Ghost, she sat glued to the pew speaking to the spirit in the ancient language of "tongues." Poppa said he looked at her and she was surrounded by an aura, like at that moment Jesus had her in His arms.

Poppa said Jesus whispered in his ear "she the one," and so it was. They married a few weeks later. Both were considered old at the time of their marriage. Poppa was thirty, and Momma was twenty-seven—too old to be starting a family, or so they thought. Poppa said I came as a gift. Momma called me a surprise. After me Momma's body couldn't hold anymore babies. She tried, but some never made it to term, some died at birth. Momma wasted away each time, so they finally gave up and spent all their time and energy on me.

Poppa did well with his church and before long bought land and built our home. Momma had a knack for hat making and was soon dressing the heads of every church-going woman in town. We were considered "colored-folks" rich and became well-respected. Momma made sure I was brought up with what she considered manners and culture. Culture was a word she had learned from Mrs. Ruby Rutledge, one of the few white women who bought her hats. Unlike Poppa, who had finished George Washington Carver Normal School, Momma had only a few years of schooling. She said she took her lessons from life and latched onto the good habits and graces of others. She insisted that I become educated, though I secretly hated school.

I inherited Poppa's looks and often felt alone—or included—because of them. I was never allowed to be just Pearlie, and I had no true friends. Momma kept me busy with piano lessons, voice lessons, sewing, cooking and serving a meal with what she called "presentation." She also made me practice how to walk in a failed attempt to take the "switch" out of my ample, naturally rolling behind. I did learn to drink my tea with my pinky finger extended, which Momma said was a true mark of a lady.

At the age of thirteen, I was baptized in the fire. Later, surrounded by the elder sisters dressed in their purest white, I tarried for the Holy Ghost. Tired, knees numb, I finally spoke and was given my earthly crown as a "saint." I became Sister Pearlie Barber, a fine example for the other young folk at Christ Temple. I was weighed down with perfection.

I went on with the life that Poppa and Momma had set out for me. I didn't allow myself to think or feel outside of what was expected. I became the church pianist, Sunday school teacher, model student and Momma's milliner assistant. Life was closed up with only room for church and family.

I finished school at age seventeen, and Momma said I was going to Teachers College up in Jackson. That summer, Momma made me a few new dresses and we had started packing the family trunk. It was becoming reality, and I was excited about the prospect of a new life. Then one morning I heard Momma whisper to Poppa that she had found a knot in her breast.

After that the prayer warriors came daily, exorcising demons, anointing with oils, and rubbing homemade salves on the egg-sized knot that seemed to have a heartbeat of its own. I watched Momma's plump body waste down to the size of a child. Her rich, brown skin turned ashen, and her eyes rolled around like marbles in her sunken face. Poppa took to his study, stumbling out late at night, disappearing into the darkness, returning early in the morning ... repeating the process the next night.

Momma lasted only six months after finding that knot. The "Saints" sent her to her heavenly home with thunder and praise. Elder Dalton delivered the eulogy as Poppa sat on the pulpit, stone still. I watched him during the service, staring at the walls of the church as if Momma's face would appear. After the service I did as I was taught: greeted guests, served food and held empty conversation—I never shed one tear. Momma would have been proud of my dignity and culture.

After everyone left that evening, I wanted to holler and tear out my hair. Instead, I cleared the dishes, cleaned up and sat in Momma's favorite chair by the parlor window. I watched as Poppa crept out of his study and disappeared into the ink dark night to his private sanctuary. I continued to sit in that chair rocking and contemplating life until the sun came up the next morning.

Life had changed in what seemed like the blink of an eye. The months came and went, and the Poppa I knew was replaced with a sour-faced man drowning in unshed tears and Mr. Percy's homebrewed white lightening. Poppa had lost his wife and his dignity. I tried to hold things together, but Momma and Poppa had only prepared me for the good. I didn't know how to handle the ugly parts of living so I turned to the church for answers.

Elder and Sister Dalton, in their wisdom, told me I needed a husband. In fact, they had someone in mind, Sister Dalton's nephew, a widower ten years my senior. They arranged for us to meet a month later after church services. He was a well-built man with regular features; full lips; a thin, nicely trimmed mustache; and dark, empty eyes. He was polite enough when we met, soft spoken, and he said he had some education. He worked at the mill and had a modest home over in Sunflower. He talked about his dead wife, who had an empty womb. He said he wanted lots of children and was looking for a young wife who could fill his house with their laughter.

I had never been allowed to court, let alone consider marriage, but I was polite. I sat there like a lady, smiling, acting interested and praying for a sign. Elder and Sister Dalton had expected me to make a decision that day, and Sister Dalton cautioned me not to wait too long. She said he was a good catch and word was that Poppa hadn't handled his business since Momma's death and was in danger of losing everything. I thanked the Daltons for their hospitality and went home, hoping I could find Poppa clear-headed enough to talk to him about the marriage proposal.

Chapter 7

Poppa had taken to disappearing for days at a time. I paced and waited. Finally, after three days, he appeared. He smelled like an outhouse and his once-broad shoulders drooped as he weaved his way over to Momma's rocker and dropped down. His frayed suspenders were the only thing that held his pants up. He had dwindled down to half the man he was. I made a pot of strong coffee and forced it down his throat, not caring that it was piping hot. I had grown too tired to be a lady.

"Poppa," I said, "I need you. I need you more than ever. We got to make some decisions."

He sat there, head wobbling, trying to focus. I kept on talking.

"I hear we about to lose everything. You always handled the family business. Do we have money? Do we own this house?"

He sat silent. I rushed on.

"It's been almost a year, Poppa. Momma's in heaven. We here—we got to keep going. She wanted me to go to Teachers College. Is there money for me to go? What are we going to do, Poppa?"

He looked at me blankly, as if seeing me for the first time.

"Pearlie, you grown now, this is real life," he said. "The money was gone before your Momma. I just didn't have the heart to tell her. Maybe if we would have had some money, she could have got good medical care, maybe she'd still be with us. I failed, Pearlie. I failed as a husband and a man of God. I can't give you no advice that would do you any good."

I was shocked. I didn't know the person who uttered those words. So I said, "Well, I guess it's settled. Elder and Sister Dalton introduced me to a widower who wants me as his wife. He got property and a decent job."

At that, Poppa looked me in the eye and asked if I loved him.

"How could I, Poppa? I just met him."

"Good," Poppa said, as he stumbled back out the door.

Three weeks later, after church services on a dreary, rain-soaked day, I became Mrs. Cleon Gipson. I felt Momma looking down from heaven and I hoped that she wasn't too disappointed because she had planned my wedding day from the day I was born.

Momma always said that she was going to make me a white dress with pearls and silk flower petals. The church would be overflowing with flowers, and I would have a three-tiered butter-cream wedding cake with kissing doves perched on top.

Instead, I married in my old, faded beige Easter suit, carrying a bouquet of cut wild flowers from Sister Dalton's garden. Sister Elroy baked a pound cake and served sweet tea after the brief ceremony. There were no gifts, and worse of all Poppa was nowhere to be found. Elder Dalton performed the ceremony and gave me away.

Cleon allowed me to go home and pack a bag. He said we would come back in a week or so and he would talk to Poppa. I cried as we pulled off down the road leaving everything and everybody I had known. Once we got out of eyeshot, Cleon looked at me and said, "Hush your bawling, woman, I ain't having none of that."

I couldn't control the tears—all the grief from losing Momma, Poppa and my life as I had known it spilled out. Through my tears, I saw the back of his hand, then was blinded by shock and pain. I tasted my own blood for the first time. I forced myself to swallow it along with spit, snot and heartache. We rode the rest of the way in silence.

We arrived in Sunflower in the middle of the night. It was pitch black outside, and I couldn't see one inch in front of me. I followed Cleon up the steps, stumbling onto the porch and fell, dropping my suitcase. He stepped right over me and left me lying there, stunned. I finally gathered up my belongings, stuffed them under my arms and trudged into the dark house. He lit a lantern and without fanfare pointed and told me to get into the bedroom.

Sister Dalton had tried to tell me in a delicate way how a woman must accept her husband, but I was not prepared. I hurriedly washed up in cold water, slipped into the pink satin gown that Momma had made for me one Christmas and crawled into bed, pulling the heavy quilt up to my neck. I waited, seized with panic. The faint light from the oil lamp cast a shadow over the dark, heavy furniture and gave the room an eerie glow.

I heard Cleon opening and slamming doors in the pantry. When he came into the room, I smelled the familiar odor of liquor. He threw back the musty quilt, looked at me, belched and then licked his lips. "You're plumper than I thought," he said. Fear crept in and I silently prayed as he unzipped his pants and snickered, "Touch my Johnson."

I recoiled and choked on a scream. He never noticed. He ripped off my gown and crushed me between the moldy, embroidered sheets. I felt searing pain as the roots of my flower were pulled away, the smell of sweat, liquor and the lingering scent of the rosewater that I had splashed on made bile rise in my throat. I breathed deeply and took myself to another place ... home with Poppa and Momma, the way it used to be.

The next morning, I woke up early. Cleon was still asleep, snoring. I inched through the house quietly, feeling my surroundings. It was a decent house, clean, which was a good attribute. I found a corner in the room, knelt and prayed. I had made a commitment before God and would love and honor my husband in spite of .... I would dismiss all thoughts of what was or what I hoped to be and live each day at a time. Through sheer determination, I would make this work. With that prayer I set about my day, starting with preparing my husband a good, hot breakfast. I had dressed, straightened up the house and had breakfast on the table by the time Cleon got up. I heard him cough up the phlegm from his throat, relieve himself and cuss as he stumbled over my shoes, which I had left beside the bed.

He made his way into the kitchen, where I presented a breakfast fit for a king: grits, fried eggs, country ham and red gravy, hot buttered biscuits and fried apples. I forced a smile as I poured his coffee. I said good morning—real sweet—as I had rehearsed. He looked at me as if I were a stranger and told me to get him the molasses from over the sink. We ate in silence. He then motioned for me to pour him another cup of coffee. I moved swiftly and sat back down.

Clearing my throat, I asked him faintly, "When do you think we can go back home? I really need to see about Poppa."

He cut me off before I could finish. "This here your home now, I heard about that pappy of yours. Think he better than everybody 'cause he got the white man's poison running through his veins. Ain't nothing no how but a drunk. Don't know when we get back there. I'll let you know."

Panic rose up and my heart threatened to come out of my mouth. My voice rose with nervousness and I said, "But I'm all he got. If I can't go there, he needs to come here." With one wave of the hand, me and breakfast was on the floor.

"Don't you never raise your voice to me, woman. Clean up this mess; you liable not to never see that ole fool again. I'm your family now. You look and feel like you ripe for children."

With those words he took me right there on the floor. I prayed that I too had an empty womb.

Chapter 8

I turned out to be a quick study. Evil now had a face: Cleon Gipson. I learned his moods and how to get around them. I also knew I had to figure out how to carve out a life for myself. Cleon only gave me money for must-haves, like food, cleaning supplies and home fixin's. I knew in order to survive, I had to escape. I continued to read my Bible, hoping for a way out.

You know that old saying: in God's own time change will come? Well, a year later change was in the making. Elder and Sister Dalton came to town for a Holy Ghost Revival. I hadn't been to church since I came to Sunflower—Cleon wouldn't allow it. He told me to pray at home 'cause church folks get into your business too much.

I knew I was starved socially 'cause I was excited about Elder and Sister Dalton's visit. I couldn't wait to hear about Poppa. I had sneaked and written him once a week. I mailed the letters when we went to the town square on Saturday mornings to shop. It had been a year, and he had not written me back, not once. I told myself he was upset that I left and just needed time.

I cooked and cleaned my hands raw in preparation for their visit. When they arrived that evening, I was reminded of how time could erode lives. Unbeknownst to me, Sister Dalton had suffered from a high fever that left her mind wandering. Most days she went back to being a child, unable to feed herself or hold her bodily fluids. Elder Dalton had aged rapidly, giving up his energy to sustain her life. Nevertheless, I welcomed them both as they represented home.

When we sat down to dinner, I watched Elder Dalton as he lovingly fed his wife the broth from the chicken and dumplings I had prepared. He wiped her mouth gently as the juice seeped from her pale, chafed lips. He patiently spooned the juices for over an hour, letting his food set and get cold. I offered to assist, but he said, "She won't eat good for nobody else." I wondered how love like that felt.

The next evening was opening day for the revival. It was a circuslike atmosphere as the workers pitched the tents and set up chairs. People from neighboring communities had come, and the women had lard heating in cast-iron skillets over open fires, preparing to fry up chicken and catfish. A group of men were on the other end of the field, laughing loud and tending the bar-b-que ribs, which you could smell for miles.

The mothers of the church sat around a table prophesying and gossiping while fanning the flies away from the cakes, cobblers and jars of jam. For the first time in over a year, I was filled with excitement and expectation. Cleon was even acting human. He had suddenly become a trustee in charge of the collection, although he had not set foot in a church since we married. While he and the other trustees were in a meeting, I roamed around, asking if anyone needed help. I dusted off a few tables and unfolded a row of chairs. Then I slipped off down the road, enjoying a few minutes of freedom.

I found a fallen tree amongst a field of golden wild flowers visited by butterflies. I sat there in solitude talking to God, with the warm sun beaming down, kissing my pale skin with color. I was sitting for nearly an hour when I felt the presence of someone. I near 'bout jumped out of my skin when I heard a voice say, "What you doing down here by yourself?"

The voice was gruff and soft at the same time. I scooted down the tree trunk away from the figure, not trusting myself to stand.

"What's wrong with you gal, you deaf?"

"No sir, ma'am," I stuttered, "just trying to get away and find some peace for a minute."

"Hmm," the voice said. "Peace for a minute? That's all you ask for? Want? Expect? You ain't asking for much."

"Well," I said, "I've learned over time that most often we don't get what we ask for."

"That may be true," the voice said, "but maybe we don't need it or we ain't asking specific enough. Well, I'm going to mosey along let you have your peace."

As quickly as the voice came, it went. For a moment I was afraid I had lost leave of my senses. Was it a ghost or a sign from God? The sun had moved and I could see more clearly. She was tall, almost as tall as Poppa, lean, the color of burnt sugar; her hair was short with natural curls. Dressed in overalls, a denim shirt and work boots, I had mistaken her for a man. I watched her until she faded from my view, wondering why my heart swelled and my mouth watered like I was sucking on rock candy.

I walked back to the center of activity, questioning who it was I had seen. I searched the crowd during and after the tent meeting but could not find her. Later that night as Cleon took my body, my mind drifted back to that golden field of flowers. The next morning, I found Elder Dalton already up and outside sitting in the rocker that I had moved out on the porch.

"Good morning, Elder, Sister Dalton still asleep?"

"Yes," he said. "She sleeps in late now-days. How was your rest?"

"Fine," I lied. I rushed on, aware that Cleon would be up soon. "Elder, I been writing to Poppa, but I haven't heard back. It's been over a year, is he alright?"

He looked at me, looked real puzzled. He stared for a long time. Then he turned his face towards heaven.

"Child, your Poppa joined your Momma 'bout a month after you left. I reckon he died from an accumulation of sorrow and neglect. I sent ya'll a telegram. Cleon sent word back that you was low sick and for us to take care of things. He sent us a few dollars to put towards his burial. It wasn't enough, but we put him away the best we could. We gave him a decent, Christian burial, though he had turned away from God."

I felt the world spinning. Later, I woke up, stretched out on the bed with a cold rag on my head. Elder Dalton stared down into my face and said to Cleon, "She gone be alright." Cleon stood over in the corner with hate dancing in his eyes. The Daltons left later on that evening after dinner.

Cleon went back to his old self and started in on me about how he had got stuck with another barren cow. I listened and watched him out of the corner of my eye as he dressed to go into town.

I silently thanked the old Indian woman I met while picking wild berries for a pie in the woods shortly after coming to Sunflower. Funny thing now that I think about it—she appeared out of nowhere. I looked up and there she stood like a tree that had come alive. She gave me a remedy for my bruised skin and told me to drink snakeroot tea to keep my womb empty. I never saw her again.

The morning after the Daltons left, I woke up feeling as though the life had been drained out of me. Cleon got up moving around like he hadn't done nothing. I was smothering in bitterness and more than once thought about feeding him poison, but all that morning I had heard Poppa's voice clear as day. "Pearlie, I sent you some protection, a lifeline, just hold on baby, watch and wait."

I moved about anxious for several weeks, and when nothing happened, I gave up. Cleon went back to the beatings and forcing. I pretended that I was not of this world. I started praying for an early death. That's the only way I saw out.

Chapter 9

Then a few months later on a Tuesday morning, Cleon woke up and said that he was going to Meridian to see his cousins about a business deal. This announcement came unexpected, and I admit I was mixed up inside. I was both scared and happy he was leaving. Was this the sign, I thought to myself? I put on my pretend concerned face and said, "How long you reckon you'll be gone?"

Cleon said, "Don't rightly know, you got someplace to be?"

"No," I said. "Just wondering .... "

Gritting his teeth, Cleon said, "You better not leave this house while I'm gone. If you do, I'll know about it."

I braced myself, expecting a knock upside my head. When it didn't come, I quickly stammered, "I'll pack you a lunch."

"Don't bother," he said, as he grabbed his hat and satchel and walked out the door, leaving his breakfast untouched.

After he'd gone, I cleared the table and walked around the house like I was seeing it for the first time. Cleon had not allowed me to change anything. It was *his* house and *his* things. He wanted it kept just like it was. When I was sure he was long gone, I started changing the furniture around. I moved the chair from beside the window in the parlor and sat it by the fireplace; I took the kitchen chairs and sat them by the window. I even tried to drag the bedroom dresser from one side of the room to the other. Exhausted, I fell asleep on top of the covers— another act that would have got me beat.

Deep in sleep, Poppa came to me again and said, "Are you ready, Pearlie?" I woke up, half expecting to see him standing there. I eased up and sat on the side of the bed, wondering what was coming next.

The next morning, the sun came up smiling. I stretched in bed and listened to the birds singing outside of my window. I had never noticed them before. After a while I got up, dressed, fixed me a cup of coffee and went out and sat on the old wooden porch swing. I stared across the field at the Hanson's place. I saw a group of people working, but I couldn't make out who they were.

The Hanson's place had been empty since the old man died. I wondered what was going on and decided to walk over to see. I went back in the house and made a fresh pitcher of lemonade to take with me so it wouldn't appear that I was just being nosey.

As I got closer, I noticed a familiar movement, a purposeful stride. Then I saw her standing lean and tall as a tree. I stopped still and watched as she led the team of workers in clearing the field. A chubby little boy noticed me first. He yelled, "Look, Miss Mattie, somebody coming." She turned and looked at me smiling, eyes gleaming. "Well, if it ain't Miz Peaceful. How you doing?"

I introduced myself proper, and we sat down under the shade of a tree drinking lemonade and talking about life. I told her about Momma and Poppa, my marriage to Cleon and how hard it was. She told me her home was Alabama but she had come here to Mississippi to take care of her aunt. Her aunt died several months ago, and she was staying on through the summer before heading home. She said she had no obligations and could hit the road any time she felt like roaming.

An hour or so passed and then she got up, stretched and thanked me for the cold drink and conversation. She said she had to get back to work. For reasons that I couldn't explain, I couldn't let her go, so I brazenly invited her to dinner. She looked at me and said, "You sure about that?"

I smiled, showing my dimples. "Yes," I said. "I'm sure."

I ran home and hurriedly put all the furniture back in place, dusted with lemon oil, opened all the windows to air the house out, cut fresh flowers and placed them in a vase in the middle of the table and started cooking. I set the table with the china that Cleon told me to never use. I bathed in vanilla-scented water and put on a freshly ironed dress with pink flowers to match those on the table. I brushed my sandy-brown, wavy hair until the natural oils rose to give it sheen and let it rest loose on my shoulders. I pinched my cheeks to get color in them and patted petroleum jelly on my lips to make them shine. Then I sat down and waited and thought about all that had happened that day.

I felt as though I had known this woman all my life or perhaps in another life. It seemed that every step I had ever taken was leading me to her. Then I thought, I can't have these feelings—this is unnatural, isn't it? Was this the protection Poppa talked about? I was so lost in thought that she was on the porch before I realized it. I opened the door and there she stood, looking like everything beautiful in life.

We talked, ate and laughed late into the night. Then she rose to go. "I can't have your neighbors talking; they probably already is. I best be getting on."

I stood wringing my hands, not knowing what to do. I did not want to see her go.

"Thanks, for the meal, Miz Pearlie. You sure is a fine cook. Take care of yourself. Remember, you don't have to be no man's whippin' post."

She touched my shoulder lightly, and disappeared into the night. I was inflamed with the fever of love.

Chapter 10

I prayed that night like I had never prayed before. Sleep never found me and I got up tired and irritable. I scolded myself, thinking, "Somebody pays you a little attention and you done lost your head. It's unnatural." I moved about the day unable to concentrate. I kept trying to read my Bible—I was sure this was a trick of the Devil.

I finally fell asleep in the early afternoon in my favorite chair by the window. I woke up several hours later, the strong smell of anise floated through the open window. I got up and opened the door. There sat a bouquet of wild yellow flowers in a quart-sized Mason jar. My Momma was the only other person who had ever given me flowers. I shed a tear and closed myself back up in the house.

Cleon came home a few days later just as he had left—mean and ornery. His business deal had gone sour, and he was blaming the world. I tried hard to stay out of his way, but just my breathing aggravated him. When we went to town that Saturday, Cleon's handprints were all over me; he liked people to know he beat me. "A real man didn't take no sass from a woman," he said.

I walked through town ashamed, head low. Cleon decided to play a game of checkers over at the barbershop and told me to wait in the truck. As I was walking to the truck, Mattie appeared.

"He do that to you?"

I nodded yes, unable to look her in the eye.

"You goin' to stay there until he kill you?"

"What else can I do, I ain't got nowhere else to go," I said.

"Yes, you do. You can come to me, be with me, like it was always meant to be. I knew it from the time I saw you in that field of flowers. God set you there for me to find."

"Mattie, you don't know that much about me, and I don't know that much about you"

"Pearlie, it don't matter ... true love is made of understanding. Understanding the other person, the object of your true love, understanding their suffering, their difficulties, and their true desires. Out of that understanding will come kindness and joy. You make up your mind to come with me and you ain't never got to worry no more. Pearlie, I would give you the breath from my body. You meet me over at the Hanson's place tonight; we be gone by morning and never look back. I'm only going to wait until sunup. If you ain't there, I'm gone."

On the way home from the center of town, I started doubting myself. My heart said go, my mind said best be sure. We arrived home and as I was taking the grocery bags out of the truck, the most beautiful pearl crescent butterfly landed on my shoulder. It sat there fluttering its yellow, green and black wings.

I remembered as a child watching Momma as she made her hats. She had explained the Biblical significance of color to me. She said yellow represented wisdom and knowledge; green was used to describe growth and how things flourished in life. Momma said even though most people said bad things about the color black, we should remember that it is always darkest before dawn. I took the butterfly as a message from Momma—it was time for me to take my life back. Poppa and Momma had given me their best. I understood what I had to do. I had to live. I had to love. I had to slip away in the middle of the night to find my way back to a flourishing life. The butterfly was a sign for me to take flight.

I went in the house and fixed Cleon his favorite meal: fried catfish, corn pone, collard greens and okra. Before he emptied his glass of liquor, I refilled it. Later that evening he fell asleep, belly full, drunk, snoring, his mouth wide open. I tiptoed around him, placing a few things in a burlap sack 'cause I dared not take time to pack a suitcase. I thought about taking the silver dollars in the cigar box that he hid under the bed. I even thought about pulling his gold teeth out of his head, but I decided I didn't want nothing that would remind me. I looked around for the last time and shrugged the weight of the world off my shoulders.

I opened the front door and crept around the back of the house. I was struck by the beauty of the luminescent, half-pearl moon against the smoke-blue sky and the silence. There was no sound except the crunch of my feet on dry land as I high-tailed it across the field, praying that the snakes let me through. I ran without my feet touching the ground ... I ran as though I had wings ... I ran for my life into the arms of Mattie Mae Lemons. We left Mississippi before dawn the next morning, and I never looked back.

Twilight

Chapter 11

The Lord allowed one of his brightest stars to descend from the heavens. She touched Earth's plane on the 23rd of February 1933, coming a month earlier than expected. They say it was a hard birthing, so hard in fact that she sucked the life right out of her Mama. Instead of celebrating new life, they grieved for the life lost.

As they prepared the Mama for burial, someone asked, what is the child's name? The Daddy said he wasn't giving her one; after all she couldn't be his. Called her a *back-door baby*. Too black to be from his seed, he said. So the Mama's sister studied the wrinkled, soot-black child with weak, watery eyes, and said her name would be Twilight. Folks creased their brows and mumbled under their breath, but the child's name and date of birth, along with the date of the Mama's death, were recorded on the faded, yellow pages of the family Bible.

The Daddy already had an outside family, so he

moved them inside the rickety shack. The rotten smell of Mama's private place still lingered in the air. Miss Annie Jane, the *other* woman, brought the daughter she and Mr. Henry had together to add to the ones he had with his now dead wife, Vertis Lee.

Now, none of her real family would or could take Twilight. Some didn't like her looks; others didn't like the fact that she killed her Mama. Some just plum couldn't afford it—too many other mouths to feed—so a neighbor took her in. The woman had been a good friend of the Mama, plus she thought it would only be for a little while.

Twilight proved to be a strange child right away. She would lay in that makeshift crib staring, cooing and just waving them puny arms and legs. Sure, normal babies do that, but she looked like she was holding a conversation with somebody. Now James and Ella Patterson, the couple who took her in, didn't mistreat her. They fed, clothed and sheltered her, but she never quite fit in with their family. They didn't hold her when she needed comfort or praise her when she did some good deed. She was just there, a permanent fixture, pretty much like a piece of furniture.

I really don't fault the Pattersons. Times were real hard back then, especially when you already had eight mouths to feed. On the other hand Mr. Henry and Miss Annie Jane was living considerably better than most. You see, Mr. Henry had a side business running moonshine across Tuscaloosa County, Alabama. Seeing them living so well and with his wife Ella's urging, Mr. Patterson decided to have a man-to-man talk with Mr. Henry to see if he wanted his child back. He thought since Mr. Henry appeared to have grieved rather quickly, he might have changed his mind. He set off across the field that evening full of courage. His wife Ella had told him what to say, but the corn liquor was telling him to say something different. He stood at the foot of the steps of Mr. Henry's now freshly painted shack and called him out.

"It seems you forgot your fistful of coal at my house. Me and Ella struggling to keep food in her mouth and clothes on her back. I see you and the Missus running up and down the road in your finery. I got Ella on my back talking about how Annie Jane keeps her hair crimped and even got a new gold tooth!

"I can hardly afford to keep food on my table—you know I got eight children of my own. You making me look bad, while I am trying to do some good. If you don't want your baby back, we can keep her. But we need to come to some figure of agreement."

Now all the while Mr. Patterson was talking, Mr. Henry stood there stone-faced, chomping down on his fat cigar. All of the sudden, he cleared his throat and said, "Just hold on a minute, I got some friends of mine I want you to meet."

Mr. Patterson stood there with his chest poked out,

thinking wait till I get home and tell Ella this, he introducing me to some of his important friends from 'round the county. He stuck his thumbs in his suspenders and tapped his feet in anticipation. He wasn't prepared when Mr. Henry presented Smith & Wesson, the shotgun that is ....

Chapter 12

Needless to say, Twilight stayed put. She proved to be a frail child, prone to fits and melancholy. Some folks even said she was touched in the head, because she was always running off into the woods and mountains. On any given day she could be seen holding a conversation with the air. The Pattersons knew she was different, but they was too busy with the daily grind of living to fret about the child's condition. After all she didn't bother nobody.

The years went on, thirteen to be exact. Everybody was into themselves, so they didn't notice the collection of bat wings, cat eyes and dried snake heads. Nobody knew that she had buried a charm filled with salt, red pepper and anvil dust bound with Mr. Henry's silvery wool hair under his front porch. They said he died of apoplexy. Nobody saw the picture of Miss Annie Jane hung upside down under the leak in the roof, where the water could drip on it. When the picture faded, she died.

Now, the Pattersons were getting up in age; they could barely get around. Their children took off for the big city, leaving Twilight behind to care for their ailments. They said it was the least she could do, 'course by then the whole county knew she was good at making medicines. They just didn't know what else she could do. They also didn't know, or care, how lonely Twilight was. Sure, she could call to the animals and talk to spirits, but what she really wanted was human, physical comfort, real family loving. So she turned her attention to her natural sisters, Essie and Henrietta.

Neither of them had two good words for her. They dared her to say she was they kin, but Twilight figured Mr. Henry and Miss Annie Jane might have soaked that in they heads. She thought with them gone, her sisters would accept her. She'd call out to them as they came down the road. Many times they'd be dressed up fancy on the way to town, riding in shiny cars. Rarely did they even look her way except to throw things. Essie even spit at her on one occasion. Twilight bided her time ....

The years went on and so did the Pattersons. Their children let Twilight stay on at the house and work the land. They were "citified" now. At twenty, Twilight still wasn't much to look at, except one time on a Tuesday afternoon, I saw her up close. She had on red chiffon, a wool beige hat trimmed in tired beaver with a pearl hat pin stuck in it. A purple, rhinestone brooch, shaped like a bird with one of its fake emerald eyes missing, held her shawl together. When she handed me a glass of water, she had crimson nails with dirt underneath and rings on each finger. She wore a watch stopped at ten o'clock on one wrist, a rabbit fur piece on the other and had animal parts around her ankles. That child had red satin slippers on her itty-bitty feet! Where was she going? Honey, she was working in her garden.

Twilight started having dreams, mainly about Tom Porter, the undertaker. He was a short, thick-necked man, had the body of a boxer. Women were fascinated by his deep-set dimples and the gap in between his two front teeth. He wore his hair parted down the middle, in perfect alignment with that gap. He had the prettiest skin I have ever seen on a man—it was the color of burlap.

Twilight was more than smitten. She was transfixed each time she saw him. She kept a constant vigil at the funeral parlor, but he never paid her no mind. He was partial to her sister Essie, who he soon married. Henrietta followed behind Essie and married Willie Thompson, who owned acres and acres of land. Fancied himself a preacher, though he never had his own church.

Twilight watched her sisters be happy, while she wallowed in misery. She had been real nice to them, though they didn't know it. She helped them get their men, even the one she wanted. You see, both men knew they were good catches so they spent a lot of time running around. Late one evening, Twilight sneaked and planted some lemon verbena around her sisters' doorsteps. That's how they really got they husbands.

Now Twilight thought about using her powers to soften hearts, but she wanted folks to love her natural. So she kept doing good deeds, tending the sick, chasing away evil spirits, and generally helping folks needing a little luck. Still, she didn't get what she was after. Folks respected and feared her, but they didn't love her. In desperation she decided to change that.

The Tom Porter dreams never stopped; in fact, they got stronger. So she decided to break up her sister's home. To do this, she had to get the tracks from Tom and Essie, taking them up while the ground was still damp. She rolled the damp earth up in a brown paper sack, along with some whiskers from a cat and a dog. Then she tied up the sack and let it stand until the earth dried and threw the whole thing into the fire. Tom and Essie could no longer get along; they fought like cats and dogs. Tom left home.

Next, Twilight made a frog charm by killing a frog and letting him dry out in the sun. She removed all the skin from his bones, and among the bones found one that looked like a fishhook, another like a fish scale. She snuck in Essie's house and stole a pair of Toms' long johns. She poked the fishhook bone into the garment. The next day he showed up at Twilight's. They were happy for a while, but she worked her roots a little too strong because Tom's extreme devotion soon proved irksome. She couldn't go off to the woods or mountains unless she was meeting somebody. Couldn't tend the sick unless he went, and she could forget going to town! She tried to dilute his loving, but it didn't work. So there she was, trapped, a prisoner of *love*.

By now, everybody pretty much knew about her powers, including Essie, but determination is a powerful thing. Essie wanted her man back. She had faith and the help of a Mississippi Hoodoo man, Uncle Poosa. She paid him ten dollars and he told her how to *"call the absent."* He also told her how to protect herself from Twilight. To call the absent, she had to pee on a piece of red flannel, rub it thoroughly on her hands, and sit down right away and write very deeply in earnest for Tom to come home. It worked. But part of him was still at Twilight's. He'd hop that fence going back 'n forth, back 'n forth, until he didn't know if he was coming or going.

Twilight took it real bad that she couldn't hold his love. Her heart was heavy from loss; her body heavy from the child growing inside her. When the time came, she was alone. Luckily, I was out walking, enjoying creation, when God decided to part the heavens. I got caught in the downpour and ran for shelter. The door was open, and there was a faint cry. After calling out I went in and found Twilight. She had bled to death.

You know, I read once that the stars are always

arriving and departing, yet the spirit is eternally anchored. The baby, a girl, was all right. She took some after her Daddy, but most from her Momma. She looked like a new moon floating in a darkened sky with wise, old eyes. While folks were arguing over whose duty it was to bury Twilight, someone looked over at me and asked what the baby should be called. I looked out of the window and there written across the sky was her name: Legacy.

Legacy

Chapter 13

Most of us view blood as an awful thing, but I've lived long enough to know that blood can both contaminate and purify—it convicts and it redeems. Some even say that blood is the gateway to the divine. Twilight made the ultimate sacrifice: her blood ensured the continuance of life.

Well, as strange as it was, Tom Porter, Twilight's unrequited lover, was the only undertaker for miles. He had to prepare her body for burial. His wife Essie insisted that he take a lock of Twilight's hair, a piece of her clothing and the one-eyed bird brooch and place these items in a hole bored in the weeping willow tree out back of the church. The hole was then plugged tightly with a piece of blessed white cloth and the red clay soil of Alabama. This was done to bind Twilight's spirit so she wouldn't return as a "haint."

I tried to tell them they were doing all that for naught

because she had left her spirit behind already. Nevertheless, to be sure, they sealed her coffin with silver screws. There were only a few of us at the graveside. Her sister Henrietta was the only family member who attended. She stood by guiltily weeping as the coffin was placed in the ground. I read the 23rd Psalm and the burial was over.

After the pitiful funeral, I pulled Tom aside and asked him one more time if he wanted his child. He puffed up like a banty rooster and said, "Ain't no child of mine could come out like dat!" Then, leering at me, he said, "You got the rest of my money for this funeral?"

Looking at him with disgust, bile rising in up in my throat, I reached in my pants pocket and handed him five wrinkled-up dollars. He unfolded the bills, pressed the wrinkles out, licked his thumb and counted. "It's all here. I guess our business is finished." He turned and walked away. I spat the bad taste out of my mouth.

At that moment, I looked up into the clouds and I swear I saw Twilight staring back. As I turned to walk away, I felt the first drop of rain, then it started pouring. Twilight was crying, hopefully for the last time.

I walked down the road home, where I knew my sweet Pearlie would be waiting for me. She couldn't take funerals, so I didn't ask her to go. Plus we had decided not to take Legacy out in the damp morning air. I came in the house after leaving my muddy boots on the back porch, walked into the sitting room, hugged Pearlie and slumped down in my Grandmother's rocking chair next to the crackling fire. Pearlie handed me a cup of piping hot horehound tea, then she knelt down and with healing hands massaged my tired legs and feet. She hummed some made-up tune as she worked the tiredness and pain from my body.

After a while, she said, "I think the baby would be much better off in the city. People around here ain't going to treat her right, and they ain't been kind to us either."

I looked down into her soft, brown eyes, and said, "Yes, you right. But Morris Bridge is the only home I know."

Pearlie said, "Home is where the heart is—think about it." It didn't take long, only a few days. One reason was I lost my job. See, I worked for Tom Porter. I guess he didn't want to have to look at me every day, knowing I had become the mother to his motherless child. To clear his conscience, he gave me my five dollars back, plus five more as a bonus for good years of service. I dragged home to Pearlie. As always, she worked her magic, cleared my mind, and we made plans.

We spent the next few weeks organizing our new life: packing, moving, unpacking and settling in Baldwin, Alabama. We found an old, rundown white-framed house that sat back off the road. Tell you the truth, it was more than a little rundown, but Pearlie quickly turned our house into a home. Shortly after we arrived, we met a "roundabout" whose name was Tuck—Pearlie called him "roundabout" because he didn't have a permanent place to lay his head. Tuck was a short, rail-thin man with burnt red skin. His appetite for liquor had tripled his age, but he could fix anything broken. In exchange for a hot meal and a pallet on the back porch, he helped me paint, tar the leaky roof and plant the vegetable garden.

A few neighbors stopped by and we talked in the yard, mainly about the weather, our gardens—safe stuff. A few went as far as to stretch their necks trying to see inside. One even made it to the front porch—but we managed to keep pretty much to ourselves. Well, as you know, necessity forces us to bring people into our lives. Our savings ran out after a few months, especially with all the work on the house. Pearlie decided she would take in washing and ironing. I went up the hill and took a job as a day worker for John Weinstein, who owned the department store in town.

We were doing alright despite our neighbors' constant meddling. See, we decided to let Tuck come live with us. That caused more talk, but it didn't matter. He fit right in, accepted us as family; no questions asked. He took to Legacy right away and was as good as any mother at changing diapers, cleaning up after her, keeping her happy. It goes to show that the roles society places on us just ain't so. In the meantime, while other people were choking on curiosity, we each were bound by a fierce, protective love.

At the end of the day, we'd all gather around the fireplace while Pearlie read to us. She was the only one with schooling beyond the fourth grade. Sometimes, all six pairs of our eyes would be fixed on Legacy as she slept tranquilly, wrapped up in my great Grandmother's old quilt, sucking her thumb, the fringed lampshade glowing with soft light shining through her translucent skin, blue veins pulsing just beneath the surface. Oftentimes, she would feel us looking down on her. The child would pop open her watery, pink eyes and coo. We'd each gently touch a different part of her see-through, silken skin and feel God.

We all admitted that we had never seen anyone the likes of Legacy, but Pearlie said she read about children born with no color. They called them albinos. Some said they were blessed with magical powers—could tell the future—but most people were scared of them, said they was the Devil's children, especially if they were supposed to be born Negro.

Since we didn't want people treating her different, we kept her close and others away. We lived in our private heaven, and things were good for a while. At the age of four, Legacy was able to read better than me and she could form her letters. Pearlie had spent her evenings teaching us. But me and Tuck were the "old dogs" that couldn't learn new tricks. Best I could manage was to write my full name in cursive: *Mattie Mae Lemons*. Tuck was double nicknamed "roundabout," but his real name was Jackson Lee Tucker. Pearlie finally gave up trying to teach him to write his name and settled for him learning to write his initials: *JLT*.

Anyway, Legacy continued to grow and learn from Pearlie. Then one day she was glued to the window watching the other children laughing and running up and down the road. She turned to us sadly and asked, "Why can't I go school? Why can't I go out to play?"

We all knew the answer, but did not know how to answer her. We had given Legacy so much of our energy and tenderness that we failed to notice when she began to change. We didn't pay attention to her melancholy, her roaming from room to room, searching. We thought her sullenness was a part of her shy nature. After all, she spent hours sitting in her corner staring into nothingness, sucking her thumb. We thought our love, our private space, was enough.

Pearlie finally said, "We'll see about it." Then she stared across the room at me with fear and uncertainty in her eyes. That night, after we put Legacy to bed, the three of us returned to the kitchen and took our places around the table. For the first time in many years, Tuck looked like he needed liquid courage. Instead, he settled on smoking one cigarette after the other. Sweet Pearlie sat fidgeting, twirling her long, sandy-brown hair around her finger, pulling it at the root, as if the pain would give her a clear mind. Me, I sat still, trying to think about what Momma Appie might have done at a time like this. In fact, I called silently to her and Twilight, asking them for direction.

We all sat well into the night, when finally Tuck cleared his throat twice as if he were about to say something important. Pearlie and me looked at him, waiting. All he could muster was, "Well, ya'll goodnight. I'm all thought out—tomorrow be another day." He got up and disappeared out into the night.

Me and Pearlie sat for a few more minutes, then she moved to turn off the lamp. She said, "I'll go check on Legacy; you go wait for me. I think you need a foot rub tonight."

Chapter 14

The next morning, we all stumbled to the kitchen table looking like none of us had a wink of sleep. You know, thinking hard is more tiresome than physical work. Pearlie, who preferred weak tea in the morning, had made a pot of coffee that would make hair grow on your chest. Me and Tuck drank ours black. Pearlie emptied the sugar bowl into her cup, which might account for what happened next.

She talked for two hours straight, wouldn't let us get a word in edgewise. She said it might be hard for Legacy at first, but she had to experience life. Said we'd all be called to glory one day, and Legacy would have to know how to take care of herself. Plus, she had the right to fall in love and if we never let her out of the house or never let anyone in the house, who was she supposed to fall in love with, a chair, table, that old clock?

She said some more stuff; in fact, she talked so long

that she stopped making sense. So I told her, "Baby, I love you but now you need to be quiet, let us digest what you said." After all that we sat in silence for a while then got up and went on with our daily routines.

That evening, it once again weighed heavily at the dinner table. Legacy picked at her food, and Tuck kept his head in his plate, like the answer was going to be found in the butterbeans. Pearlie sat staring at the tiny hole in the kitchen wall where there was once a rusted nail and last year's faded calendar.

I couldn't take it no more, so I said, "It's decided. Legacy, you now eight years old; it's time we let you get a feel for the real world. We kept you between these walls, only letting you go out in the backyard once in a while. You ain't never seen beyond that there fence. It ain't right, though we thought it was.

"Well, tomorrow is Sunday, and I guess the Lord's Day as good as any. Instead of having our private church in the sitting room like we always do, we all going to get dressed in our best and go on down to the church on the other side of the hill. I hear that preacher can make you kick up the dust."

Legacy came out of her trance; the child jumped up out of the chair and danced around the table, hugging us so hard our eyes were about to pop out. Old Tuck took his head out of his plate and started playing hambone on his bony thighs. Pearlie grabbed the tambourine off the mantel and started keeping time with Tuck. I joined in after turning the kitchen drawers inside out looking for my harmonica. Chile, we were all singing and "cuttin' the rug" as my Momma used to call it, tears streaming down our excited faces. At that moment we had all come to life.

Sleep didn't come easy though. We were all dead tired from our coming out party. I reckon we were all thinking about what lay ahead. Pearlie got up early and ironed all our clothes. She had bathed and curled her hair—her curls sat in neat rows cooling before she combed them out. She had breakfast cooking, and the smell of coffee, burnt hair and fried bacon choked the air. I got up, opening windows.

Silently walking into the kitchen, I watched Pearlie like I had seen her for the first time ... skin the color of fresh-churned buttermilk, her plump body wrapped in a pink chenille robe. She looked like a fresh cut rose. I watched her for a few minutes unnoticed, then she turned away from the stove, smiled and said, "Good morning love. We ready for the day?" I nodded yes, not quite sure.

Pearlie called out to Legacy thinking she was still asleep. She wasn't. She was up, washed and dressed in a faded blue dress a size too small. Pearlie inspected her, smelled under her arms, had her blow in her face and sent her back to the bathroom with a sprinkle of soda in her hand to brush her teeth. When she came back, Pearlie greased and combed Legacy's coarse, bleached hair and tied a pink ribbon on each of her four plaits. She also had her change into a pretty, pink flowered dress that she had sewn.

Tuck came in from the porch. He had shaved and brushed his few strands of hair into place. He looked right nice in his fresh white shirt and starched overalls. He even spit shined his old cowboy boots. Pearlie took the opportunity to fuss at me for not owning a dress, but I never found them necessary. I did draw a half smile of approval when I stepped out of the bedroom in my freshly starched white shirt, vintage Mexican silver bolo tie and stiffly creased black pants. Tuck surprised me as he handed me my rundown penny loafers that he had put a shine on.

We all sat and tried to eat the biscuits, bacon and eggs that Pearlie had prepared, but all we could manage was coffee. Legacy forced down a half glass of milk at Pearlie's insistence. Pearlie cleared the table and grabbed the tattered family Bible that we kept at our bedside. We all piled into my old '49 pickup and headed over the hill.

As we drove up the dusty road, we could hear the congregation from a quarter mile away. "*Blessed assurance, Jesus is mine! O what a foretaste of glory divine! Heir of salvation, purchase of God, born of his Spirit, washed in his blood...*"

Lord, I hadn't heard that song in years. Me and Pearlie stopped going to church years ago. To be more honest, we were asked to leave because of what others called our "ungodly ways." Pearlie took it harder than me 'cause she was active in the church—choir, sick visitation and such. I told them old hens that if God is love, then he recognizes all kinds of love and I love Pearlie.

Legacy brought us all out of our private thoughts with her squealing. The child was so excited; I thought she would go into a fit. We pulled onto the dusty road and parked. Pearlie inspected us all. She patted her curls back into place, tugged at Legacy's plaits and ran her hand over my short, coal-black hair. We were ready. Holding each others' hands, we all marched up to the front door of the church. Tuck let loose of my hand to open the heavy oak door. Straining, he held it open as we all walked in. At that very moment a strong wind came out of nowhere and slammed the door shut. All heads turned towards us, the singing stopped, and I heard a woman gasp. Pearlie halted, but I pulled her along. We cleared a pew as people scurried away.

The preacher stuttered for a moment, but got himself together, greeting his flock and the new visitors. He preached that morning to a silent crowd. After the benediction, people almost ran out the door into the dirt yard. We let them pass, then I walked up and shook the preacher's hand and told him I enjoyed the service. In fact, I did. Tuck slept through most of it, with Pearlie nudging him whenever he started to snore. Pearlie looked peaceful, and Legacy, she was just plain happy. The child could sing!

We never knew that before. Reverend Wallace, as he introduced himself, shook all of our hands and welcomed us to come back. He told Legacy that he would love to have her in the choir. She smiled shyly and hid behind Pearlie. We told him we'd be back soon.

Chapter 15

As we walked to the truck, we noticed the people staring, mouths gaping open. Pearlie walked nervously, smiling and bowing her head in a "howdy do" to each one. They didn't smile back. Legacy kicked at the gravel not paying anyone any attention until someone said, "Wonder what marked that child?" She looked at me, questioning. All I said to them was time to go.

Legacy talked more on the ride home than she had in all her eight years, and she had taken notice of everything: a hat a woman was wearing that looked like our flower garden, an older boy who was making faces at a young girl in the choir and the picture of white Jesus with his heart exposed behind the pulpit. Legacy shocked us all by asking if her mother the color of Jesus. We had told her about her mother Twilight when we thought she was old enough to understand, though we didn't tell her everything.

Pearlie cleared her throat and said we all look like

Jesus, our Heavenly Father, and that he made us all in his image. Legacy, being a bright, questioning child, said, "If that's so, Aunt Pearlie, then why we all look so different?"

That caught Pearlie off-guard for a minute, but she said, "You know the flower garden that Tuck and Mattie planted? Well, in it there's all kinds of flowers—tall ones, short ones. And different colors—red, orange, purple and yellow—all beautiful. So, you see, God had a lot of work to do creating the world, and he would have gotten bored if we were all the exact same. So he gave each of us our own quality; each of us got something wonderful to offer to the world. We all got our own part of Jesus."

That seemed to satisfy Legacy at that moment. We continued to ride; everybody seemed happy but me. Well, I had butterflies in my stomach. Something just wasn't sitting right, but I didn't want to put grits in the Vaseline so I smiled and hummed "Blessed Assurance" along with Legacy, Pearlie and Tuck.

When we got home, Pearlie fixed us a grand supper and we all ate like it was our last meal. Full, all the grown folks retired to the parlor. Legacy ran around the house gathering up school supplies.

"Uncle Tuck, where is that cigar box? I need it for my pencils. Momma Mattie, I might need a new tablet. Aunt Pearlie, what am I going to wear?"

She went on like that for hours. Gathering up her "school materials" as she called them. Finally, at sunset,

Legacy tired herself out. Pearlie told us to wait up for her while she washed Legacy up and put her to bed.

After we knew she was asleep, we talked again. Tuck said, "You know it's going be hard for her. You heard those people today, and they was church people." I sat quiet puffing on my pipe, thinking. Pearlie agreed that it may be hard at first, but said, "She such a beautiful child—they'll see after a while."

"Ok, here's the deal," I said. "We're going to try this school thing out, but if they hurt my child's' heart and Lord help him if they harm her physical ..."

Pearlie got mad then and said, "We need to stop it! Think positive. She's going to live, be normal, be loved just like everybody else. We so concerned about what everybody else think. Ask ourselves what we think—the way we carrying on we telling ourselves and the world that something *is* wrong with that child. Ain't nothing wrong with her but she needs and wants love. We're going to pray tonight. Then we're going to get up in the morning and take that child to sign up for school."

Morning came fast. We all ate a quick breakfast of oatmeal, dressed and headed down the road. Legacy looked like sunshine in her bright yellow dress, her hair plaited with yellow ribbons weaved in. Tuck surprised us all and made her a lunchbox with beautiful hand-carved flowers and her initials, L.L., for Legacy Lemons.

We got to the school early on purpose, before the

school yard filled up 'cause we didn't want people staring. Plus, Pearlie insisted that we not be late. Hillger Elementary School was a little red brick building with small glass windows in the front. The property was fenced in with a playground that had a swing set and sliding board. Legacy laughed and sang as we entered the doors.

The halls were empty, but we walked in the direction of voices. We entered the office as two women sat talking. I remembered one from the church. She turned, looking surprised, then put her face back in order.

"Well, good morning. I'm Mrs. Wallace. Who do we have here?"

"Mrs. Wallace," I repeated.

"Yes, Reverend Wallace's wife. I am the principal here," she said.

Pearlie said under her breath, "God works in mysterious ways."

"Well, Mrs. Wallace, this is my adopted daughter Legacy Lemons. We been schooling her at home, but she's smart as a whip. She can read better than any of us, count, figure and write in cursive. She got a natural gift for learning," I said.

Mrs. Wallace looked surprised. "You mean to tell me this child has never been to school?"

"No ma'am," I said. "We kept her home safe—maybe us grown folks need to talk in private."

Mrs. Wallace told the other lady, Mrs. Smitherman,

the school secretary, to show Legacy around. They left the office, then we talked. I told Mrs. Wallace about Legacy's beginning and what we thought of as her "condition."

Mrs. Wallace said that she might get some teasing. Children do that, but she would get it under control and not allow anyone to hurt her. She said she needed to test her to see what grade she would be placed in since she had never been to school. She told us to go on home; she'd be in good hands and come back at 2:45 to pick her up.

We left, though we didn't want to. Pearlie cried all the way home, and Tuck set his face in worry. I dropped them off, telling Pearlie to hush up all that crying and to take some Stanback headache powders and drink a Coke-a-Cola. I knew that would knock her out for a while. Then I said, "Tuck, look after her. I'm going to work. I will stop by and pick up Legacy after school."

I went on back down the road, parked the truck behind some trees and walked back to the school. I found me a spot where I could sit and watch—just in case. I sat there all day until the bell rang.

As the time neared, I walked into the schoolyard. I watched as children poured out of the building laughing, talking loud. I looked for Legacy, but she wasn't there. I saw a group children peering into the office window. As I walked closer, I heard them chanting "peeled potato, monkey face, ghost!" My footsteps on the gravel alerted them, and they ran off, laughing. I looked in the window and there sat my baby, sobbing, her face buried in Mrs. Wallace's lap. Sensing my presence, Mrs. Wallace looked up and nodded for me to come inside.

"Legacy has had a rather rough day," she said. "She is not used to interaction with others. I'm afraid that keeping her isolated has slowed her social skills."

"Talk English," I said roughly. I was already aggravated and didn't want to hear no big words.

"I'm sorry," Mrs. Wallace said. "What I meant is she is used to you and the people in her house. Apparently, you did everything for her, and she does not know how to fend for herself. Don't worry, she'll get used to the other children, and they will get used to her. It takes time. Bring her back tomorrow, and we'll get a fresh start. She tested well above her grade. She can be double-promoted."

"Well, I told you when I brought her here that she was smart. Pearlie saw to that, and she got some of it natural. Her mother, rest her soul, was touched by God. She could learn anything. She even knew what animals were thinking."

With that, Mrs. Wallace looked kind of puzzled, but she put her principal face back on and said, "And don't worry, I will also deal with those bullies. I won't have that at my school."

After our talk I gathered Legacy in my arms. She was limp as a wet dishrag. I wiped her tears away and took the end of my shirt and told her to blow her nose. For the first time my baby had color. Her eyes and skin were blood red. A chill ran up my spine as I thought she looked just like the Devil.

When we got home, Tuck and Pearlie was sitting on the porch waiting. One look at Legacy and they knew the story. She walked right past them as if they were not there and went in the house to her room.

"They give her a hard time," Tuck said, half questioning. "Well, we knew it was most likely to happen."

"Yes," said Pearlie, "but she made it through the first day. She be stronger the next."

I stood listening, then said, "I don't think she should go back; she smart with your homeschooling. Mrs. Wallace said so. Said she tested well past her grade. Said something about she didn't have no social skills though. I think she's wrong about that. We taught her to respect people; she got good table manners."

Pearlie moved over on the porch swing, motioning for me to sit down. Then she said, "I don't think that's what she meant, Mattie. I think it was just what we talked about; we kept her too protected. She got to develop thick skin, learn how to function in the real world. She's going back tomorrow and that's that."

In all our years together, sweet Pearlie never talked to me like that. Though she ruffled my feathers, I let it pass. I would make my feelings known again in the morning.

Well, to make a long story short, morning came and off we went again. The days turned into weeks, the weeks into months, and the months into years. Pearlie was right—people did learn to love Legacy, and more important, Legacy learned to love herself. That girl was into everything: the choir, social clubs, volunteering down at the old folk's home. We were all happy and proud, then just as sure as the seasons change, so does life.

Chapter 16

Her screams woke us all up in the middle of the night. Confused and panicked, we all ran into the direction of her room, nearly knocking each other down. When we opened the door, there she sat on the side of the bed. Though the child naturally didn't have color, she had turned transparent white. I swear I could see her heart beating, the red-and-blue lines pumping blood through all her organs. She looked like the picture I had seen in her science book of a man with no skin showing all his innards. She was breathing hard and fast, and Pearlie screamed for me to find a paper bag.

I ran into the kitchen and came back with it. She held it to Legacy's mouth and told her to breath slow. Pearlie sat and held her, rocking and singing her favorite song. *"Just when you feel that you are all alone, and when you feel that your love is gone—just remember what I say for every word is true—you have everything—when you have Him ..."*

After a few minutes what little color Legacy had came back, and she started breathing normal again.

We all asked at the same time what was the matter with her. She said that she smelled perfume, and when she opened her eyes, a woman was sitting at the foot of her bed. She said she had never seen her before, but she looked familiar. Said she remembered she had on a brooch shaped like a bird—it had one emerald eye, but the other was missing. Me and Pearlie looked at each other, knowing. Tuck ran into the kitchen to get his hidden bottle from under the sink.

Years ago, Twilight had told me that the bird was a gift from God. She said that as a child, the bird guided her when she was in the wilderness. It showed her what herbs to blend for sickness and spirits; it taught her how to live off the earth. One day, a hunter saw the bird and decided to kill it for its assortment of feathers. He shot it in the eye, killed it dead and stripped it of its feathers. Now to tell you the truth, the story was strange because I ain't never known of a rainbow-feathered bird to be prancing free in the woods of Alabama. She went on to say that the dead bird resurrected and flew onto her shoulder and turned into that brooch. From then on she had the ability to see beyond the sun.

While I was reminiscing about Twilight, Pearlie brought me back to the present by asking Legacy, "What did the woman say to you, baby?"

Legacy said she told her that danger was coming, and they needed to leave the house in the morning. She said not to question, just believe. Legacy was really agitated, eyes darting to-and-fro and wringing her hands. We finally quieted her, and she went back to sleep.

Pearlie made a pot of her sacred tea. We gathered around the table, thinking to ourselves. Tuck finally said what we were all thinking. "Wonder what she want? What she trying to warn us about?"

Pearlie said, "Mattie, what you think we oughta do?" Before I could answer, she said, "Well, I'm not leaving my home."

Thinking back, I knew and should have followed my first mind. Instead, I worried about leaving my home goods behind.

It started as a drizzle during the night, but by morning you could not see what was in front of your face. The storm's rampage claimed lives and ravaged property throughout Baldwin County. Our house and others along the road flooded. Some people managed to stuff pillow cases with staples—potatoes, sugar, salt. We escaped with nothing but our lives, trudging through stale water, mud and other garbage, dodging snakes and insects to get to high ground. We finally made it to the church, where people were packed like sardines. The heat and stench was unbearable. Reverend Wallace was there ministering to distressed souls in spite of the fact that Mrs. Wallace was missing. I heard him tell somebody that wherever she was, he knew she was with the Lord. Others were not as confident.

Chapter 17

The storm raged for three days and three nights. Pearlie lay damp and feverish for most of those days. Tuck joined the rescue team, disappearing into the night; he wouldn't be seen until weeks later. The town's only colored doctor, Old Doc Brown, was working to save the lives of the severely sick. Legacy, guided by the whisperings of Twilight, took care of everybody else.

She said Twilight told her: *For the fever, make a mixture of flour and vinegar. Smear it between two rags and wrap it around both feet and put their socks back on. Take that raw egg still in the shell—rub it all over the body. It'll absorb the heat from the fever. The egg will be as hard as if you cooked it—don't eat it—draws out all the body's poison. Mix rectified turpentine with sugar for the hard cough. Use salt vinegar and barley water for that sore throat.*

Legacy moved between the pallets and cots rubbing, massaging, forcing fluids down people's throats. Me and some of the other church sisters followed her, praying and laying on hands.

None of us slept through those stormy nights. We lay awake listening and wondering what was in store for us next. Then on the last night of the storm, I fell into a hard, dreamless sleep. The next morning, I woke up to stillness and sunlight spilling between the cracks of the plywood that was nailed where the stained glass windows once were. Soon others rose and we all stood looking towards that stream of light. It was as if God was calling us. I was the first one to open the door of the church, and waded out a few feet, carefully, awkwardly. I cried because before me were downed trees, vacant lots where houses once stood, and the road leading to the church was completely washed out. God had sent us a message.

Days after the storm, the river continued to belch up bodies, all total fifty people, men, women and babies, lost their lives. Setting things back to normal in Baldwin took toil and sacrifice. People were reunited, and we grieved for those lost forever. Finally, we cleared trees, patched roofs, and made makeshift passages until the roads were repaired. The cleanup took months, but nobody was without a roof over their heads. We took in homeless strangers and amid the gloom people came together as one. Legacy was instrumental in that. She not only had the power to heal the physical, she could renew people's spirit, make them have the will to carry on. She was young but old at the same time. I worried that she was missing out on a normal sixteen-year-old's life. But Pearlie said, "Leave it alone, Mattie. God ain't going to give her more than she can handle. This is her purpose." And so it was.

The years continued to unfold, you know time and life don't wait for nobody. Legacy grew into a fine woman. Went to Tuscaloosa Junior College, and took up nursing. She knew more about healing than the teachers and doctors, but she said she needed the legal papers to practice. While going to school, she met Rayfield Loving and fell in love. Yes, that is his real name. He was going to school to be an engineer.

Tell you the truth, at first I wasn't too excited about Ray, that's what we call him. He was a few years older than Legacy and always talking about moving up North. But after a while he grew on us, and Legacy was happy. So on a beautiful, cloudless day in the month of May, Legacy Lemons became Legacy Loving. When Reverend Wallace said, "I now pronounce you husband and wife," there was a cloudburst that lasted for less than a minute. Then the sun came out, and an arc that looked like it reached from here to heaven appeared. I told Pearlie, "That's Twilight crying tears of joy."

Well, Ray eventually took Legacy up North to Detroit. He found work at Ford Motor Car Company, and Legacy became the first colored nurse supervisor at Mercy General Hospital. God gave Legacy an empty womb but an overflowing heart. They adopted three little girls whose parents were killed in an accident. For the most part they all turned out good, except one—that Peaches is the bad seed. Anyway, Me, Pearlie and Tuck lived a good life.

We lost Tuck first—his liver gave out due to all that drinking that he had done in the past. Before he died he opened up and told us about his life. Ain't that something, we all got a story.

Pearlie lived to be eighty-two, though her mind drifted away long before. She came to herself the night before she died, told me she was going home in the morning, and would be waiting to rub my feet. I smiled and kissed her on the forehead and said, "You do that baby." She died during the night in our bed in my arms, smiling.

Legacy and Ray had been fussing about Pearlie and me living in the house alone. We always told them that we ain't alone when we got each other. Now I couldn't say that anymore, and the house felt so empty. So I gave in, but not before making them both promise to bring me back to Baldwin when I die and bury me between Tuck and Pearlie. They said they would, and I trust them. So I packed up my personal belongings and sold or gave away everything else except our four-poster bed and my family quilt.

The night before Ray and Legacy drove down to pick me up, I walked through the house, storing memories in my heart and mind. That morning, my neighbors were waiting for me in my front yard. There were tearful farewells and keepsakes as I said goodbye to my life in Baldwin. Now I live here with Legacy and Ray on the east side of Detroit on Langley Street. I have seen over a hundred years—don't know how much time I got left. One thing they can say for sure when I go to my final resting place: "Mattie Mae Lemons left a legacy of love."

Tuck

Chapter 18

I can't say death snuck up on me. I feel like I've been dying for years, but each time I rallied and kept myself going. This time though, the doctor says it won't be long ... days ... weeks ... a month at best. I got a lot of stuff floating through my head. Sort of like an old record that keeps playing after you try to turn it off. They say I'm in a coma, but I can hear everything being said and I can still think.

To be exact, I can think back almost to the time I was born in Fairhope, Alabama. My Momma and Daddy were sharecroppers, worked Ole Mr. Tom's land. Me and Mr. Tom Whitmore had the same great-granddaddy. Daddy learned me and my brothers Hershel and James to work with our hands, to work the land. I didn't take to school, though Momma kept up such a ruckus about us going. My brother James made it to the ninth grade; Herschel, the baby, finished high school, went to the army, came back and went to college. As for me, well I made it to the fourth grade. Daddy said it was no use in me going to school. Momma cried but knew better than to complain too much. I took my education from nature and went to work in the fields; I learned about land, seeds and moon planting. I took pleasure in tilling the soil and watching things grow. I learned to fix farm equipment and anything else broken.

Daddy got the consumption when I was thirteen. James had already married and had his own place in Prichard. Herschel was useless, kept his head in a book, so it was up to me to keep things together and provide for Momma. I took care of the land and Momma until she followed Daddy over the River Jordan about a year later.

Me and Mr. Whitmore never hit it off. See, I knew he was cheating folks even though I couldn't keep figures. I told him so. He pulled a shotgun, so I pulled a knife. I had to run across fields and rivers ahead of the lynch mob. I felt scared because I left Herschel behind. He said to go on, that he'd be alright, and I found out later he was. Some folks liked his mild ways and protected him and made him their houseboy.

Anyway, not knowing where else to go, I ran to my brother James. He had made good for his self. He was a preacher and had a job at the pecan factory. James married the most beautiful woman in all of Alabama. Her name was Lillie Ruth Jenkins; she was the color of butterscotch and just as sweet. When she smiled, there sat dimples deep enough to swim in. And her eyes, well, they talked all by themselves—she never had to open her mouth. That's how I knew she loved me as much as I loved her. I didn't go after her deliberate. To be exact, I made a point to hound around trying to find a replacement for my affection. I couldn't. No one compared. I sidestepped her touch, wouldn't even take the spoon she handed me over the dinner table. I figured it held her pulse, her scent. I told myself to move on, get out of the way of the trouble that was surely brewing.

Then something happened to set things in motion. James was asked to preach over in Saraland. Said he was hoping that they was considering him as the replacement for their preacher of twenty-five years who had dropped dead while visiting a sister on the sick and shut-in list. Just days before he left, Lillie Ruth took sick with the grippe. James debated on leaving her as all her people lived way up in Grove Hill—it would take them forever to get there. And the church people, well, they probably would bring a few food baskets, pray and such but wasn't too many going to empty slop jars, change fever-drenched clothes, wash and change sheets, and such.

I stepped in and told him to go. I would find a woman to come in and help. I could handle everything else. When I said it, I had Clara Bell Franklin in mind. She hung out at Sippy Flats Café drinking, crying broke and talking about how hard it was to take care of six kids with no husband. So I went down the road and brought her back to help. That lasted all of two days.

I caught her stealing. She had her children running in and out of the house, each one taking something with them, so I told her to go ... not so nicely. She stood there with her flat-foot, wide-hipped self cussing me for being born and accusing her, a "God fearing" woman, of stealing. As she marched towards the door, a sack of rice fell from under her dress. She went to kick it under the bed, hoping I wouldn't notice, and a bag of brown beans that she had held between her ample thighs busted and scattered across the floor. She ran out of her shoes down the road, and I rolled across the floor dancing on them beans.

After that mess I decided to take care of Lillie Ruth myself. I bathed the fever away and got her to take some chicken broth. In three days she was able to sit up in bed and plait her hair by herself. On the fourth day she was able to move around the house a little bit. On the fifth day I looked into her eyes, and they told me she needed me as much as I needed her. James was gone Sunday-to-Sunday. When he returned just after sundown, me and Lillie Ruth had gone too far to turn back.

We didn't set out to do harm to nobody. We told ourselves that it wasn't right, but our hearts overruled our heads. We took every chance to connect—a slight touch of our hands as we passed along a piping hot bowl of grits at breakfast, arms rubbing together as we carried the clothesbasket to the line, a brush of our feet under the dinner table. Eventually, our accidental touches became deliberate, and Lillie Ruth would make excuses to go out into the woods.

"Sure would be nice to have a boysenberry pie, think I'll go out and pick some. Tuck, you want to come help?"

Off we'd go. James never suspected; he was busy pacing back-and-forth, practicing his sermons. He had been asked to come back in two weeks to preach again. Lillie Ruth feigned sickness to stay behind. James fussed and said the congregation would have to meet and spend time with her to see if she fit the role of a first lady. Lillie Ruth coughed harder and turned red-faced with each word. Finally, James gave in after she promised that short of death she'd go with him the next time. So off he went.

We was free like little children. We danced, played and loved in the moonlight. We got so caught up, we got careless—though we wouldn't find that out for months later. Seems that old Clara Bell and Willie T had been out in the woods looking for boysenberries too. They seen and heard us—stored the information for later.

Well, to make a long story short, James got his preaching job and came back to get Lillie Ruth. It took a month or so for them to pack up, and I noticed during that time that she was more quiet than usual. I figured we both was trying to think how we would tell James about us. I had asked her already to spend her life with me. She said she would always be with me, and that was good enough.

Then one evening at the dinner table, I looked at her real hard and noticed that her color wasn't too good and her eyes were dark and sunk in. I waited until we was alone and asked her, "Honeybones, is you alright?"

She burst into a flood of tears. "I got a baby growing inside of me, Tuck. What we going do?"

I grinned from ear-to-ear and said, "We gonna be a momma and daddy? I got money saved under the mattress. I can take care of you and the baby. We can get us a little place; I'll find regular work." I went on and on, not noticing her strange look.

Finally, she said harshly, "Looka here, Jackson." She called me my formal name. "You a fine man in your own right, but you ain't the settling type. You'd never make me the kind of home James will. You can't raise my station in life. I'm getting ready to be a first lady. What would I be to you?"

"You'd be loved," I said. "Loved and taken care of. That's all God intended for us."

"What we did is against God, but I'm going to fix it," she said. "I got to try and figure out how to make James think this baby is his. We ain't been together as man and wife for a while. His mind been so occupied with getting this preaching job."

She paced back-and-forth, then stopped short. "I

know what I can do. When it comes time, I'll say the baby came early. I'll eat just enough not to get too big before it's time. I'll ... "

As she was plotting, my heart was coming through my mouth in pieces. I was blinded by rage. I left her sitting there talking to the air and plodded down to Sippy Flats Café to kill my pain with brown liquor, the old water of life. It stirs your thinking, and I had to think about what I was going to do next.

Clara Bell was there, as usual. She slid her ample self over to me and asked if I would buy a friend a drink.

"Who is my friend," I asked.

"I could be. I could be a *very good* friend," Clara Bell said. "After all, you and me got secrets."

I bought her a round of drinks to shut her up. My mind was racing, and the liquor wasn't working fast enough to dull my pain. I ordered a bottle, killed it and ordered another. Clara Bell sat licking her lips at the second bottle. Then she said, "A plate of Sippy's red-peppered pig feet and tails sure go good with that liquor." I ordered her two plates. She ate, smacking, spittin' bones and lickin' her sticky fingers. Then she said, "You ackin' like a man got his heart broken."

I told her to mind her own business, but she kept on. "What happened, Miz Lillie Ruth got full of you? Decided you ain't the cat's meow after all?"

I hates it when people dig at you, so I told her, "Shut

up, Clara Bell." But she kept on.

"Yes, she always been high and mighty. Got her eyes set on being a first lady. James most likely can take her places. You can't take her nowhere but on the soft ground in the woods."

She laughed loud, teasing me. The liquor and anger boiled up and over and I lashed out. I saw a flash of red, felt a crunch, teeth flew in my face, and before I knowed anything, Clara Bell was sprawled out on the floor, her dress almost over her head. Her eyes were floatin', and she was mumbling and trying to swallow the blood that was seeping from her mouth.

In another split second I saw a flash of light, felt scorching pain and then darkness. I woke up two days later in the storeroom of Sippy's place—head bandaged so that only my eyes showed through. Sippy came in and told me I got cut up pretty bad by Willie T. Said Clara Bell was alright though she'd only be suckin' food for a while.

Then he said, "You better stay here where you safe. Your brother James looking for you, and he told someone he gonna kill you sure. Look like you in a heap of trouble and too weak to fend for yourself, lost a lot of blood. Might of lost your pride and family too."

I stayed in that storage hole for two months. Sippy, who had learned medicine during his stint in the Army, patched me up as best he could. Willie T had cut me from the top of my left ear, across my nose, taking a piece of nostril, down across my upper lip and up again to the tip of my right ear. I said the scar would forever remind me of the trail of my life's mistakes. In a matter of weeks, I lost everything: Lillie Ruth, my baby, my brother and my face. I thought about going back and trying to connect with my baby brother Herschel, but I heard his life was so different now, and how could I explain what I had done? So I packed my belongings in a rucksack and walked the roads, stopping here and there, trying to carve out a life.

The wind carried the message that Lillie Ruth gave birth to a beautiful little girl. She was born with a clubfoot. Lillie became the grand first lady of Prince of Peace Baptist Church—just like she dreamed of. She would forever own my heart, and I wanted her to be happy. I made up my mind to forgive but never forget. I knew I would never love another woman. To make sure, I learned to numb my feelings with liquor.

During those years, I lived off the land. I learned to require little and want for nothing. All my worldly possessions fit in one bag. Along the way, I lived with people but not off people. There is a difference. I took, but I gave back. I learned from others and taught others too. I wasn't an educated man, but with my teachings, children learned to carve animals out of pine tree stumps, men learned to build houses, fit pipes for plumbing and tar roofs. I taught widow women to grow their own food even when the soil was sand or clay. I used what God gave me to help change people's lives ... trying to right my past sins. That's how I found Mattie, Pearlie and Legacy.

Chapter 19

I roamed into Baldwin around 1945, though I didn't meet Mattie and Pearlie until a few years later. I was stumbling down the road late one evening, full of cheap bourbon and self-pity, wondering about Lillie Ruth and our baby girl, who was school-aged by now.

I ran into Willie T during my travels. That Willie T sure could build a story. He told me that James and Lillie Ruth was living "high on the hog." Both had filled out; they lived in a big, fine house that would take up a city block. James drove a long, black Cadillac that was a gift for his pastor's anniversary. They didn't have no more children, but doted on their daughter Barbara Jean, who favored her mother except for her long, hawk-like nose. When he said it, he stared at me for a moment, wondering if the piece of mine that was missing made the puzzle complete.

I'm sorry, I drifted .... Anyway, as I was saying, I was stumbling down the road when I heard a woman cussing up a storm about leaking roofs and such. Another woman yelled out the window for her to watch her mouth, said people might be listening. Although I heard two women's voices, the person I saw looked like a man from behind—had on overalls, flannel shirt and a brown, sweat-stained Stetson pulled down over her eyes. She must have felt me lookin' 'cause when she turned I could clearly see it was a woman. She was tall, reed thin, with dark, piercing eyes and beautiful doeskin. She placed her hands on her hips and spread her legs slightly apart in a wrestling position. She's protecting her territory, I thought, so I quickly said, "Sorry ma'am, didn't mean no harm."

She didn't say anything, but I could feel her staring at my back as I walked away. Two days later, I was hauling my wagon collecting what other people call junk. It's funny that I could fix, polish and sell back to people what they throwed away—just goes to show how wasteful we can be. Anyway, as I was hunting for stuff there she was again, up on the ladder fixing on the roof. I said, "Howdy ma'am," loud, on purpose. She looked up from what she was doing and nodded her head in a greeting.

"Hard work, ain't it? If you had a little help, might go faster." I seen she was making more work for herself than need be, but I knew better than to say it. So I said, "I got a few minutes, won't charge you nothing."

I didn't wait for her to say anything—I just started climbing up the side of the house. Pretty soon we was working side-by-side, never saying a word. After an hour or so, I heard another voice.

"Mattie, come down. You need to eat, get out the sun, come down now, you hear."

Mattie grunted, gathered her toolbox and for the first time looked me in the eye and said, "You welcome to stay for supper." I couldn't remember my last home-cooked meal. I had been living off cold canned beans.

We climbed down and walked to the back porch. Mattie looked at me and said, "You got to take them boots off. Pearlie raises hell about marking up her clean floors."

We both left our dirty boots side-by-side on the porch. We walked through the screen door into the kitchen. The sight and smell of buttermilk cornbread, beef stew, apple cobbler and fresh brewed coffee made tears come to my eyes. My mouth was watering so bad I had to wipe it with my sleeve. I hoped they didn't notice.

The plump one smiled like sunshine and said, "Hi, my name is Pearlie Gipson. If I know Mattie, she ain't introduced herself proper. She Mattie Mae Lemons. Welcome to our home."

I shifted my feet and looked down at the floor, all of a sudden aware of what I looked like. The scar, the dirty clothes, the caked dirt under my nails though I had just washed my hands.

"My name Jackson Lee Tucker. People call me Tuck," I mumbled.

"Well that's a strong name, Tuck. Have a seat," Pearlie replied.

We all sat down around the kitchen table. Pearlie served Mattie and me heaping helpings of thick gravy stew with seasonings I had never tasted before. I said, "This stew is fit for a king, Miz Pearlie."

She smiled, showing dimples, reminding me .... "It's my momma's secret recipe," she said.

I ate two big bowls of stew and half the pan of cornbread. I was too full for the cobbler and was trying to figure out how to ask for some to take with me when I heard a baby cry. We all looked in the direction of the noise at the same time.

"Legacy waking up hungry," Pearlie said as she got up from the table and walked to the next room. Mattie stood up and said harshly, "Time to go."

Pearlie heard her and said, "Mattie, that's not nice. His food ain't digested yet. Plus, we got cobbler and coffee. I'll just feed Legacy and get her quiet. She'll go right back to sleep."

I was thinking to myself, Legacy, what kind of name is that for a child? And these two women living like man and wife—I had heard tell of women that went after other women down at Sippy's, but this was different.

Anyway, Mattie and me sat at the table silent until Pearlie came back. She fixed us bowls of the cinnamon-laced cobbler and coffee and asked me a hundred questions: "Where you from, Tuck? Where you live around here; what kind of work you do; do you have family?"

Mattie half-heartedly scolded her once or twice about "asking the man his business," as she called it, but that never slowed Pearlie down. She kept asking, so I answered without answering, to be polite.

It was getting on into the evening so I said, "Thank you, Ma'am, for your hospitality. I best be getting along." With that I got up and left, though Pearlie insisted on giving me a bag of cold chicken and the rest of the cornbread.

Days later, I found some temporary work down at Cooper's Mill. It ran for two weeks; regular work back then was far and in between. Cooper had a shanty for his help, and hot meals were served once a day. The watery stew didn't hit a lick at Miz Pearlie's, but it kept me going. I had to wean off liquor too if I wanted to keep working.

Two weeks went by fast, and I was back to scrapping. I was walking the roads again when I passed their house and noticed they had dug up a spot for a garden. I heard singing as I walked up to the fence. There sat Pearlie rocking a cradle, staring out at nothing. I cleared my throat loud, so she would notice me without being scared away.

She looked up and smiled. "Well Tuck, where you been? We were wondering about you. Come on in, sit for a spell. Mattie went to town to pick up a few things. I got dinner on. You like pinto beans?"

"Yes ma'am, I do, but I don't want to put you out no kind of way. I just stopped by to say hello."

"You ain't putting us out. Tell you the truth, I like the company. We just rattle about in this house—it gets lonely sometimes without the outside world."

I looked at Pearlie strange, not understanding. The baby was awake and cooing, though I couldn't see nothing but movement under the blanket. Pearlie looked at me real hard, then said, "Tuck, I suspect you understand 'bout people being different. I felt it the first time we talked. Don't think you fooled us by half answering my questions. One day you will trust us enough to open up."

She was tapping on my heart and mind. I said, "Some things best to forget, not talk about. I just learned to live day-by-day, Miz Pearlie. I don't set roots nowhere; it's best not to get attached."

She had taken the cooing, wrapped-up bundle out of the cradle. She slowly removed the blanket and a set of pink eyes looked up at me. I swallowed hard as I stared at the ghost child. Pearlie said she was born like that, but was growing normal like any other baby.

"Why ain't she got no color?" I asked.

"We don't rightly know," Pearlie said, "except God made her that way."

We sat there soaking up the sun, and she told me

about Twilight, the child's natural mother. How they come to take Legacy and send her to some state home. Her daddy Tom wanted to sell her to the circus people. Mattie stepped in, and her and Pearlie became Legacy's Momma and Daddy. We talked and talked; she invited me in while she finished cooking, even handed me Legacy while she took the bread out of the oven. I hadn't held a baby since my brother Hershel—it felt strange and right at the same time. I thought about my baby girl ....

'Bout the time she finished frying the chicken, Mattie drove up. A flash of aggravation danced across her face when she saw me.

Pearlie nervously started talking. "Me and Tuck had a fine day. He told me how to treat that clay soil to get our garden growing. He watched Legacy while I got some things done."

With that, Mattie exploded. "What you mean he watched Legacy?"

"Oh calm down, Mattie," Pearlie said. "They were never out of my sight. He's good with her, see?" With that, she picked Legacy up out of her cradle and dumped her into my arms. On cue, Legacy cooed and smiled, arms and legs dancing to some unheard rhythm.

Mattie stood over us and smiled at Legacy. "I guess she take to you alright. Let's eat. I'm hungry."

Pearlie placed another fine meal on the table. We ate, then settled in the parlor listening to the radio, talking about life—especially the young folk who were starting to stand up for our people throughout the South.

Finally, Pearlie said, "Tuck, since it's so late why don't you make a pallet out there on the porch. We'll see you in the morning."

That was that. I became a member of the family. We built upon this house. We took care of one another, and we raised Legacy. Now Legacy grown and married, done moved away. Life changes, you know. We all old now, and God done decided to call me home first.

I done asked for forgiveness of my sins, and I had Pearlie write James and Lillie Ruth a letter.

Dear James and Lillie Ruth:

Hope this letter finds you both well. I am low sick. The doctor say ain't long. It's been over thirty years since I seen you but I hear tell you did well. Got a big church, big house, raised a big, beautiful girl who is now a full-grown woman with her own family. I didn't forget you ever and did not mean to hurt nobody. I never knew love could creep up and steal your soul as well as your heart. Forgive me and we see each other again across the river.

Love,

Your brother, Tuck

P.S. I did not grow old alone. I got me a family too.

Epilogue

"Momma Mattie, what are you doing out here this time of morning? How'd you get out here all by yourself? Come on now, don't give me a hard time. Let's get back in the house before you catch a death of cold. I swear most days you can't hardly walk from the bed to the chair in your room. Now you have made it clear out here on the porch all by yourself. You could have fell and bust your head open, broke your hip, anything."

"Hush up fussing girl, I heard Pearlie calling me and I got up trying to find her. I followed her voice out here."

"Momma Mattie, now I have told you a hundred times about that. Pearlie been gone for years; you just had a bad dream that's all."

"Legacy, it weren't no bad dream—I heard her clear as day. When I made it out here on the porch, all three of them was smiling at me from that full harvest moon."

"All three who, Momma Mattie?"

"Pearlie, Tuck and Twilight—all three of them was smiling and waving to me. Pearlie say she still waiting for me, got us a nice place over on the other side of that moon. See it? You know that they say the moon is the peaceful home of the good dead."

"Now, Momma Mattie, be careful not to blaspheme. You know all saints go to heaven."

"Legacy, where do you think heaven is? The moon what we see is the gateway. It represents peace and gentleness."

"Well, Momma Mattie, it don't look like I'm going to be able to get you into the house no time soon, and we don't want to wake up Ray. He has to be at work at seven o'clock in the morning and needs his rest. Here, let me wrap you up in this quilt and we'll sit here for a while. You're right, the moon sure is pretty, and I've often wondered what lies beyond the sky."

"Legacy, I believe our loved ones never leave us. In fact, I know they don't. I talk to my peoples all the time on the other side. On special nights like this, they even let me see them."

"Let you see them? Come on, Momma Mattie, you're starting to worry me."

"No need to worry, just stating a fact. They appear—sometimes they take a seat on the dangling end of the moon. Sometimes they dance around the moon, and sometimes I just see the shadows of their faces looking through it."

"I see, I suppose there isn't any use in trying to convince you otherwise."

"No chile, it ain't. I know what I know. It ain't goin' to be long for me, Legacy. Ain't goin' be long now."

"Hush, Momma Mattie, you probably outlive us all. Dr. Paddock said you have the health of a sixty-year-old.

You just troubled with 'ole Arthur' like most of us that's over fifty. And you and Ray both need to stop eating pork to get your blood pressure under control."

"No, babe, that ain't all. I'm tired and my body done told me it won't be long. Pearlie calling me more often; she lonely, tired of waiting. I also talk to your momma Twilight—she's so proud of you. Do you remember her story? I think you need to hear the stories one more time ... so you can remember when I'm gone.

"I'm like the world's oldest living tree, like the one they wrote about it in the newspaper last week. I believe they said it was something called a Norway spruce. This group of science people found it in the mountains of Sweden. They believe it's lived to be near a thousand years old. No, I'm not quite there, though I'm a hundred and two and counting. Like that old tree, I'm hanging on and ain't lost my senses yet.

"I've been through a whole lot in this life, Legacy, but the Lord gave me insight and the ability to withstand rough times. Yes, he built me strong. I could work as hard as any man, but I'm soft as cotton inside. I've loved a lot over the years. My sweet Pearlie—we were together over five decades. You know we can't help who we love.

"Then there was Tuck and Twilight and you, my dear Legacy, you is my child though I didn't birth you. You the only one left of my loved ones. I know you got your own family now, your own struggles. But Pearlie, Tuck and Twilight ...

"Anyway it don't matter now 'cause they all long gone, but each of them left a piece of their life with me. Now I just live off my memories. I guess that's why the young folk on Langley Street call me the storyteller. They say I'm wise, got intuition, can see how to take everyday problems and make use of them for the good. They also laugh at my stories, but not at me. There's a difference, you know. I tell them each of us got a story to tell. Some are grand, bigger-than-life stories, some are funny and some, well, just plain sad. I believe that while each of us has our own history, each account is important in its own way.

"I know these life experiences were lessons for me, and they helped to shape who I have become.

"Yes, I am a storyteller ... lived to be one hundred and two."

Critical Commentary

Dancing Under the Same Moon is rich with vibrant characters who jump off the pages and compel us to revisit our recent past as women who have been tormented, forgotten and scorned, but most of all, as ones who rise above it all and like a phoenix take on the meaning of life and transform it into love.

The Mt. Vernon Hospital for the Negro Insane is a metaphor for our life that is all too lyrical, tragic and at the same time funny. Readers will find themselves crying, laughing and remembering what makes us so special and complex as women of African descent in America.

This work of fiction has the simplicity of a griot's story that made an Alice Walker novel come alive, and the beauty of J. California Copper's tapestry that pulls from our diaspora as Amazon African tribal women who survived horrendous oppression many times at the hands of our own men and certainly under the white power structure. She also has the sophisticated focus of mysticism found in Toni Morrison's work while elevating spirituality, along with common sense, and mother wit to describe the many characters we see every day in black women.

Debraha Watson has a unique voice that advances our understanding of "how we roll as black women" and makes our voices so critical to the survival of our humanity.

Portia Hunt, Ph. D., Professor of Counseling Psychology at Temple University

About the Author

Debraha Watson is a poet, short story writer and essayist whose work has appeared in *Black Hair: Art, Style and Culture*; *Material Feminism*; *It's Worth the Struggle: Inspiration for Contemporary Writers*; *Paradise Valley Days*; *Days Dawn;* and *Reverie Midwest African American Literature*. She is also a former senior editor for the Detroit Black Writers Guild.

The writer holds a Ph.D. in Adult and Higher Education from Capella University in Minnesota; a Master of Arts in Adult and Higher Education from Morehead University in Kentucky; a Master of Science in Administration from Central Michigan University; and a Bachelor of Applied Science from Siena Heights University.

Ms. Watson uses her personal experiences and knowledge of social and political reform to assist those in society who have suffered abuse.

Made in the USA
Charleston, SC
12 October 2010